Eva had noticed him before, of course. And recognized him. What woman wouldn't notice this dark and broodingly handsome man, or recognize him as being one of the wealthy and powerful Greek Lyonedes cousins?

His looks didn't hurt, of course. Eva stood five-eleven in her three-inch heels, but Markos Lyonedes was still several inches taller. Tall enough that he could look down at her with warm and broodingly sensual green eyes.

"I hope you'll excuse my coming over and introducing myself?" He quirked dark, questioning brows over his enigmatic green eyes. "I'm Markos Lyonedes."

Even his voice was sexy, Eva acknowledged—deep and husky, with an undertone of dark and sensual. The sort of voice guaranteed to send a shiver of delight down women's spines.

Other women's spines, Eva corrected firmly. Fortunately she was totally immune to conceited men like Markos Lyonedes. Most especially to Markos Lyonedes himself. "I know who you are, Mr. Lyonedes." Just as she knew exactly *what* he was.

The Lyonedes Legacy

Nothing—and no one—dares to stand in the way of
these Greek tycoons

With the strength and allure of Adonis, these two Greek
cousins stand proudly at the head of their empire.

Their Achilles' heel?

Beautiful women.

July 2012

Defying Drakon

Drakon Lyonedes is accustomed to having any beauty he
wants, but Gemini Bartholomew proves a surprising challenge

August 2012

His Reputation Precedes Him

Markos Lyonedes, the charming rogue,
conceals a will of steel every bit as forceful as his cousin's!

Carole Mortimer

HIS REPUTATION
PRECEDES HIM

HARLEQUIN®
entertain, enrich, inspire™

Recycling programs
for this product may
not exist in your area.

ISBN-13: 978-0-373-13085-6

HIS REPUTATION PRECEDES HIM

All about the author...
Carole Mortimer

CAROLE MORTIMER is one of Harlequin's most popular and prolific authors. Since her first novel, published in 1979, this British writer has shown no signs of slowing her pace. In fact, she has published more than 135 novels!

Her strong, traditional romances, with their distinctive style, brilliantly developed characters and romantic plot twists, have earned her an enthusiastic audience worldwide.

Carole was born in an English village that she claims was so small that "if you blinked as you drove through it you could miss seeing it completely." She adds that her parents still live in the house where she first came into the world, and her two brothers live very close by.

Carole's early ambition to become a nurse came to an abrupt end after only one year of training, due to a weakness in her back, suffered as the aftermath of a fall. Instead she went on to work in the computer department of a well-known stationery company.

During her time there, Carole made her first attempt at writing a novel for Harlequin. "The manuscript was far too short and the plotline not up to standard, so I naturally received a rejection slip," she says. "Not taking rejection well, I went off in a sulk for two years before deciding to have another go." Her second manuscript was accepted, beginning a long and fruitful career. She says she has enjoyed every moment of it.

Carole lives "in a most beautiful part of Britain" with her husband and children.

Other titles by Carole Mortimer available in eBook:

Harlequin Presents®

To absent friends

CHAPTER ONE

'I thought the meeting earlier with Senator Ashcroft's aide went well...'

Markos Lyonedes took one last look at the late afternoon New York skyline from the eightieth-floor window of his office before turning to look at his PA, his expression rueful. 'Yes?'

Gerry gave him a quizzical glance as he stood on the other side of the imposing mahogany desk. 'Didn't you?'

Markos moved back into the spacious room. His dark suit was tailored to fit perfectly across muscled shoulders and chest, lean waist and long, powerful legs. He honed that fitness at the moment with early-morning runs in one of New York's parks. Aged thirty-four, he was a couple of inches over six feet, with dark, slightly over-long hair, and shrewd green eyes set in a swarthily handsome and chiselled face indicative of his Greek heritage.

He gave the other man a steady glance. 'That depends upon whether Senator Ashcroft would have sent his aide or come himself if Drakon were still in charge of the New York office.'

Just a month ago Markos had been based at the

London offices of Lyonedes Enterprises, the company he owned with his cousin Drakon, with a full and busy business and social life, and no thoughts of moving to New York. That was before Drakon had met Gemini, the London-based Englishwoman he was to fall in love with. Drakon and Gemini had become engaged and were married just two short weeks later. The two of them were even now on their honeymoon on the Aegean island owned by the Lyonedes family.

Luckily Markos and Gerry had instantly found a rapport, and Drakon had already expressed his approval of the PA Markos had taken on at the London office, following a rather embarrassing episode for Markos with the young woman who had been his previous PA. Just thinking of the way she had thrown herself at him during the last business trip they'd made together was still enough to make Markos shudder.

'Drakon had already accepted the Senator's invitation. He must have forgotten to mention it with all the wedding arrangements,' Gerry dismissed. 'Senator Ashcroft obviously wished to make sure that the new head of Lyonedes Enterprises, New York, was aware of the invitation. And he didn't send just *any* aide to extend the invitation—he sent his only son!' Gerry gave a grin. He was a tall, rangy man in his late thirties, with sandy-coloured hair and a pleasant rather than handsome face.

Markos raised dark brows. 'That's good?'

Gerry's smile widened. 'The Senator is grooming Robert Junior to take over when he retires in a couple of years. And invitations for the event on Saturday evening are being coveted like bars of gold by New York society. My wife would kill to get one. I thought your offhand acceptance of the invitation was pitched about right,' he added approvingly.

'It was actually caution on my part—because I wasn't sure if I was being insulted or not.' Markos gave a grimace as he sat down behind the desk. 'I'm afraid American politics remain a complete mystery to me.'

'All you need to know about most of our politicians is that re-election is their main goal, along with gathering up the necessary finances to run a successful campaign. That's why the Senator's schmoozing the New York head of Lyonedes Enterprises. This company employs several thousand New Yorkers, and thousands more all over the world.' Gerry gave another grin.

'That's a pretty strong incentive for the Senator—' He broke off as a knock sounded on the door before Markos's executive secretary entered the office.

Lena Holmes was yet another invaluable employee Markos had inherited from his cousin. A woman in her late forties, slightly plump and motherly in her plain dark business suits, she nevertheless succeeded in running Markos's office with the precision of a sergeant-major in the English army.

'Sorry to interrupt, Mr Lyonedes, but I thought I should let you know straight away that Ms Grey has cancelled her five o'clock appointment.'

Again, Lena's disapproving tone implied.

Evangeline Grey, interior designer extraordinaire— if her reputation was to be believed—and the woman Gerry's wife had recommended for redesigning the rooms in the penthouse apartment above them, had already cancelled one appointment earlier in the week.

'What was her excuse this time?'

Lena's mouth tightened. 'An emergency appointment with her dentist.'

Markos glanced at the plain gold watch on his wrist and saw that it was already five minutes to the appointed time of five o'clock; if Evangeline Grey had intended being here for their appointment this evening then she should have left her downtown office some time ago, not cancelled five minutes before she was due to arrive.

'It must have been a very sudden emergency...'

'I wouldn't know, Mr Lyonedes.' Lena expression remained disapproving. 'She asked if she might reschedule for Monday evening at five o'clock instead.'

'What did you say?'

'I told her that I would return her call on Monday morning and let her know if that time was convenient for you,' Lena reported with satisfaction.

'And is it?'

'You currently have no other appointments at that time,' she conceded.

Markos smiled ruefully. 'But it won't hurt to let her think about it over the weekend?'

'Exactly.' Lena nodded.

'Thanks, Lena.' Markos waited until his secretary had left the office and closed the door firmly behind her before turning to look questioningly at Gerry. 'That's the second time Evangeline Grey has cancelled on me in a week.'

The older man turned up his hands. 'I have absolutely no idea what's going on there. Kirsty thinks the sun rises and sets on the woman's interior designs. And I have to admit I thoroughly approve of the innovations she made in our bedroom six months ago...'

Markos quirked mocking brows. 'Do I want to know what they are?'

'Probably not, as Kirsty is now four months pregnant!' Gerry chuckled before sobering. 'Do you want me to see if she can recommend someone else?'

Lyonedes Tower, both here in New York and in London, had a penthouse apartment occupying the whole of the top floor of the building. Markos had never taken up residence in the apartment in London during the ten years he had been based there, preferring to live away from his place of work—just as Drakon had preferred to own an apartment in Manhattan for the time he had lived and worked in New York: an apartment he and Gemini had decided to keep for the times when they visited.

Having only arrived a week ago, and finding the apartment above this office to be both convenient and spacious, with fantastic views over the skyline of New York, Markos had thought it best to make it his home until he felt more settled. He had decided to call in an interior designer with the intention of having it decorated more to his personal taste. Evangeline Grey was that interior designer.

The apparently elusive Evangeline Grey.

He gave a dismissive shrug of his shoulders. 'Let's wait and see what happens on Monday.'

'Phew, am I glad you said that!' His PA grinned good-naturedly. 'I would really hate to disappoint Kirsty. She likes the woman so much that before you even asked for the name of an interior designer she was thinking of trying to arrange a dinner party so that she could get the two of you together,' he explained at Markos's questioning glance.

'If she cancels the next appointment that may be the only way the two of us ever meet!' Markos leant back in his high-backed leather chair. 'For some reason the name Evangeline gave me the impression she was an older woman...?'

Gerry shook his head. 'Late twenties, I think.'

'Really?' His brows rose. 'Isn't that young to have built up the professional reputation she has?'

The other man shrugged. 'If you haven't made it in New York by the time you're thirty then you're never going to!'

Markos smiled slightly. 'Is she attractive?'

'I was always out at work when she came to our apartment, so I've never actually met her.' Gerry frowned. 'But I'm presuming so, if Kirsty wanted to introduce the two of you.'

Markos gave an appreciative grin. 'In that case let's hope that she actually manages to get here on Monday evening!'

Gerry nodded. 'If only to save me from suffering the brunt of Kirsty's disappointment! Although there will be plenty of beautiful women for you to meet at the Senator's party tomorrow evening.'

He gave a weary shake of his head. 'I think I've probably already been introduced to every beautiful woman in New York over the last four days!'

'You haven't met Kirsty yet!'

Markos grimaced. 'Being surrounded by all this love and romance is bringing me out in a rash!' First Drakon and Gemini, and now Gerry had made no secret of the fact that he was very happily married. 'As I now unexpectedly have an hour free, why don't we go through the last of these contracts?'

The elusive Evangeline Grey was already dismissed from Markos's thoughts as he instead concentrated his attention on the work he wanted to get finished before beginning his weekend.

A weekend which now seemed to include spending his Saturday evening at Senator Ashcroft's drinks party.

For some reason Markos had felt slightly restless since moving to New York. Of course the two weeks before the wedding had been frenetic, followed by his lethargy after flying to New York only a day later. His arrival had been quickly followed by one meeting after another as Markos introduced himself to the company's extensive business associates, and there had been a social function of some sort for him to attend every evening as New York society opened their homes and welcomed him to their city in place of his cousin Drakon.

Maybe the change-over had happened so quickly that Markos still felt slightly wrong-footed by the unfamiliarity? This office. The apartment on the penthouse floor above this one. The new people Markos worked with every day, and the others he socialised with every evening.

Whatever the reason for his restlessness, Markos knew that attending yet another party tomorrow evening was the last thing he wanted to do…

Eva had never enjoyed cocktail parties, having been forced to attend far too many of them in the past. She enjoyed those given by US Senators even less. All of the city's rich and beautiful were filling to capacity the huge reception room at one of New York's most prestigious hotels. The chatter was loud, the laughter even more so, and the jewels adorning the elegantly clad ladies' wrists, throats and ears glittered and sparkled in the light given off by the dozen or so crystal chandeliers hanging overhead. At the same time Eva's senses were being assaulted by the smell of dozens of expensive perfumes filling the air-conditioned room.

But, as her mother had been so fond of saying, 'What can't be cured must be endured.' It had certainly been true with regard to her marriage to Eva's father...

It was taking all of Eva's endurance to grit her teeth and get through this cocktail party hosted by none other than visiting Senator Robert Ashcroft. Not because she thought there was a risk of meeting any of her ex-husband's family—she knew from mutual friends that Jack had taken over the family's Paris office just over a year ago, and her ex-father-in-law, Jack Senior, didn't support Senator Ashcroft's political party. No, there was no possibility of her meeting any of Jack's family this evening.

Even so, Eva doubted she would have bothered accepting the Senator's invitation if she hadn't known how much it would appeal to the man who was her date for this evening. It was exactly the sort of social function Glen enjoyed. Which was fine. It just wasn't the real reason she had wanted to see him again.

In truth, Eva had no idea how Glen was going to react when she found the opportunity to explain that she had absolutely no intentions of going to bed with him—ever—or with any other man, for that matter. Instead she was thinking of asking him if he would be the sperm donor if she went ahead with the IVF she was considering. A subject so delicate, so personal, was something she felt she had to lead up to slowly, rather than blurting it out at their first—or even second!—meeting.

Senator Ashcroft's drinks party was turning out to be every bit the crush of people Markos had expected it might be. Most of them were already known to him after this past week of socialising, and a lot of the men wanted to renew their acquaintance with him. Their wives, daughters or girlfriends were making no secret of the fact that they found his dark and brooding looks attractive.

Not that Markos had any complaints about that last part. He had enjoyed a healthy sex life during his years of living and working in London, and he sincerely hoped to continue doing so now that he had moved to New York.

Nevertheless, even surrounded by beautiful women as he was, all seemingly vying for his attention, Markos still noticed the woman in the figure-hugging red gown, standing across the room...

Probably because she stood out from the rest of the 'beautiful people' present in as much as she was making no effort to respond to the flattering conversation of the half a dozen men currently surrounding her, but instead seemed totally bored—both by them and by her surroundings.

But it wasn't just that air of uninterest which had captured Markos's attention. Nor was it the fact that she was young—probably in her late twenties—and extremely beautiful. Ebony hair cascaded lushly over her shoulders and halfway down her spine, and her eyes were light in colour—possibly grey or blue?—and surrounded by thick dark lashes. Her skin was the colour of pale alabaster, her features delicately lovely, and the fullness of her lips was glossed the same tempting red as that utterly decadent gown. Her only jewellery was a pair of delicate gold filigree earrings which dangled almost to the bareness of her shoulders.

All of that would certainly be enough reason for any man to give her a second glance, but still it wasn't what had caught and held Markos's attention, what had caused his body to harden in instant arousal the moment he looked at her.

Every other woman in the room wore masses of expensive jewels at their ears throat, wrists and fingers and, whether tall or short, they were all fashionably slender—a look that wasn't flattering to some of the younger women, and even less so to most of the older ones. The woman in the fitted red strapless gown wore only those earrings, and her figure was...

There was a word for her type of figure. An old-fashioned word that described her exactly—one that had often been used to describe movie stars of the golden age... Voluptuous! That was it! The tall woman in the red fitted gown was voluptuous. Not fat—her body was too obviously toned for that. She simply had an hourglass figure: curvily, lushly, sexily voluptuous. The sort of body, in fact, that most men preferred but so rarely found in this fashionable age of slender and willowy.

Her shoulders were bare, that expanse of skin the same smooth alabaster as her face, and that wickedly enticing gown enhanced the fullness of breasts that were obviously bare beneath the silky material that swept over her narrow waist before clinging lovingly to the sweet curve of her hips. The material finished a couple of inches above her knees to reveal long and shapely legs, with three-inch heeled red strappy sandals on her elegantly slender feet.

Markos's breath now caught in his throat as she looked over the top of the heads of the men surrounding her, glancing around the room in obvious uninterest—almost as if she was aware of someone watching her, but had no idea who or why. His earlier impression of her complete boredom with her admirers and her surroundings was confirmed as she repressed a yawn. At the same time as their glances met.

Met and then, as the woman's gaze shifted slowly back to his, held.

Markos quirked a questioning brow—only to receive a blank stare and then a uninterested shrug in reply, before the woman in the red gown, as Markos was already calling her in his mind, turned away to accept a fresh glass of champagne from one of the men surrounding her, to all intents and purposes as if she had already forgotten Markos's existence.

While it might be a refreshing change after the past week and this last couple of hours of having women throw themselves before him like sacrificial offerings, this certainly wasn't the reaction Markos was used to receiving when he showed an interest in a beautiful woman.

As one of the two Greek-born Lyonedes cousins, with business interests worldwide, and wealthy beyond imagining, Markos had never been naïve enough to believe it was his looks alone which attracted women to him. Nor did he believe that every woman he met had to find his height and dark looks attractive.

But still, it irked him that the woman in the figure-hugging red gown—a woman who made him hard just from looking at her!—had dismissed him so easily and completely.

Maybe she was married?

Or engaged?

Or perhaps in a serious relationship?

No, it certainly wasn't either of the first two; the hand holding the glass of champagne she had just raised to those lush red lips—her left hand—a long and slender hand Markos could all too easily imagine moving caressingly over his much darker skin in a pastime his arousal also approved of as he felt his shaft throb in anticipation!—was as naked of jewellery as her throat and wrists. And if it was the latter then where was the man she was involved with?

If a woman as beautiful as that had belonged to Markos then he certainly wouldn't have left her alone for a minute, at the mercy of the pack of hyenas currently in for the kill.

If a woman like that *belonged to him…*?

What the hell?

Markos didn't do belonging. Or even long-term. And definitely not permanent.

A few days, in some cases a few weeks, of enjoying each other's company—and bodies—was the limit of any interest he had shown in the women he had been involved with over the past eighteen years.

Liking—yes.

Sex—definitely yes.

Love or belonging—definitely no.

His cousin Drakon—a man who had been even more averse to permanent relationships than Markos until he'd met Gemini a month ago, and fallen so quickly in love with her—might have succumbed to commitment to one woman, but Markos certainly wasn't interested in doing the same.

He *desired* the woman in the red gown. He was more than a little annoyed at the ease with which she had dismissed him just now. At the same time as he was aroused and hard just from looking at the way that fitted red gown clung so lovingly to all those voluptuous and below the gown naked curves. It was an arousal Markos knew he would prefer *her* to satisfy, rather than another woman's willing body.

It was with that thought in mind that Markos distractedly made his excuses to the women crowded about him before crossing the room towards the woman in the red gown.

CHAPTER TWO

GOLD.

Markos had been wrong about the eyes of the woman in the red gown; they were neither blue nor green, but so light a brown they appeared a deep shade of amber gold.

A deep, glowing and unfathomable amber that swept over Markos in cool uninterest even as the men gathered about her took one glance in his direction before parting to allow him to reach the woman's side.

Like Moses parting the Red Sea, Eva noted ruefully as the men around her instinctively stood aside for the tall, dark and arrogantly handsome man who had deliberately caught her gaze a few minutes ago before making his way so determinedly across the room towards her.

She had noticed him before, of course. And recognised him. What woman wouldn't notice this dark and broodingly handsome man? Or not recognise him as being one of the wealthy and powerful Greek Lyonedes cousins? Certainly Markos Lyonedes's photograph had been all over the New York newspapers this past week as he attended one social function or another.

His looks didn't hurt, of course. Eva stood five

eleven in her three-inch-heeled red sandals, but Markos
Lyonedes was still several inches taller. Tall enough
that he could look down at her with warm and broodingly sensual green eyes.

His dark hair was inclined to curl over his ears and
nape, and his emerald-coloured gaze was now narrowed
and assessing, set in an arrestingly handsome face that
looked as if it might have been carved from mellow
gold stone: high and hard cheekbones, a long blade of a
nose, chiselled lips, and a square and determined chin.
The perfectly tailored black evening suit did little to
hide the fact that he was also powerfully built—wide
and muscled shoulders and chest, flat and tapered abdomen, lean hips, and long, long legs.

No doubt about it. When it came to charisma and
good-looks, Markos Lyonedes had it in spades!

It was perhaps unfortunate—for him—that Eva
knew Markos Lyonedes to be exactly the sort of man
she wanted nothing to do with. Personally or professionally. Which hadn't precluded her having a little fun
at his expense this past week…

'I hope you'll excuse my coming over and introducing myself?' He quirked dark, questioning brows over
enigmatic green eyes. 'I'm Markos Lyonedes.'

Even his voice was sexy, Eva acknowledged. Deep
and husky, with an undertone of dark and sensual. The
sort of voice guaranteed to send a shiver of delight
down women's spines.

Other women's spines, Eva corrected firmly.
Fortunately she was totally immune to conceited men
like Markos Lyonedes. Most especially to Markos
Lyonedes himself. 'I know who you are, Mr Lyonedes,'
she said. Just as she knew exactly *what* he was.

The dozen or so men who had been vying for her attention seemed to have recognised that he was a man to beware of—if for different reasons than Eva's—and had now drifted off to a safe distance, leaving the two of them completely alone in a room full of the richest and most fashionable people in New York.

'You do?' His brow arched questioningly.

She gave a smile of rebuke. 'All of New York society—and most especially the women!—is agog with the fact that Markos Lyonedes has recently arrived in our midst!'

Markos studied the voluptuous woman in the clinging red gown through narrowed lids as he detected the mockery beneath her smoky tone.

Her beauty was all the more apparent now that Markos was standing next to those deep amber-coloured eyes, the perfect nose, the full and sensuous lips above a pointed chin. Her alabaster skin had the fine smooth appearance of porcelain in the bareness of her shoulders in the strapless gown.

And she was most definitely naked beneath that gown!

Well…her breasts certainly were. The berry-like nipples were temptingly outlined against the silky material, the perfect fit of the gown over the fullness of her hips surely only allowed for a pair of gossamer-thin panties. Panties the same vibrant red as her gown? And would they be made of lace? Or silk?

Markos drew in a deep breath as his already hot and aroused shaft gave a throb of response just at the thought of his seeing this shapely woman wearing only a pair of brief and silky red panties.

'And you are…?'

'Eva.'

His smile was teasing. 'Just Eva?'

She gave a light inclination of her head. 'Just Eva.'

The coolness in her voice, as well as her demeanour, was really starting to irritate—and arouse!—the hell out of him. 'It's a pleasure to meet you, Just Eva.'

The sensual fullness of her lips curved into a chiding smile. 'Shouldn't you get to know me a little better before deciding that?'

'Well, I already know that you're English,' Markos murmured slowly as he finally heard her speak more than two words together

That enigmatic smile widened, revealing white, even teeth. 'Obviously.'

Yes, definitely mockery, Markos noted wryly, even as he wondered at the reason for it. It usually took a beautiful woman a lot longer than two minutes' acquaintance to decide he might be dangerous.

He nodded. 'Having just lived in England for ten years, English is an accent I've become familiar with.' An accent, he now realised, that he had sorely missed this past week.

Eva gave an acknowledging inclination of her head. 'And how are you enjoying New York?'

He shrugged broad shoulders. 'Well, so far I've realised that it truly is a city that never sleeps.'

That was one of the things Eva had come to love about New York since she had moved here seven years ago. At the time she had been twenty-two, fresh out of university and newly married to a native New Yorker. Her career had instantly blossomed, and the city of New York had 'taken'—but unfortunately the marriage hadn't. She and Jack had separated after only four years, and divorced not long after. That experience, and her own parents' less than happy marriage, had left Eva with the viewpoint that once bitten was twice shy—and with the intention of never marrying again.

She shrugged. 'Oh, come on. If nothing else you have to appreciate the fact that you can buy a decent cup of coffee here any time of the day or night.'

Smoky green eyes warmed in sensual invitation. 'I've found that the percolator in my apartment makes an excellent cup of coffee. Day or night...'

'Wow.' Eva looked at him admiringly. 'It took you... what...? All of five minutes' acquaintance before inviting me back to your apartment.' She went on dryly at his enquiring look, 'Surely that has to be a record, even for you?'

Markos stilled, now positive that he hadn't been mistaken about the sharp edge of derision that seemed to underlie every word this woman said to him. '"Even for me..."?' he prompted softly.

She shrugged those bare shoulders, the movement drawing attention to the full and creamy swell of her breasts above the neckline of the silky red gown. 'I'm afraid your reputation has preceded you, Markos.'

'And what reputation might that be...?'

Amber-coloured eyes looked up into his unblinkingly. 'Why, that you're as lethally single-minded in your pursuit of a woman you desire as you are cold and calculating when it comes to ending a relationship.'

Markos straightened, his lazy humour fading in the face of her attack. 'I beg your pardon...?'

Had she gone too far? Eva wondered with an inward grimace. After all, circumstances might be such that she was predisposed to dislike and disapprove of

Markos Lyonedes, but having now met him there was no doubting that he was a force to be reckoned with in New York—both professionally and socially. Just as his cousin Drakon had been before him.

She had met Drakon Lyonedes twice, both times only briefly, and had found him to be a much different man from his slightly younger cousin. Just as handsome as Markos, Drakon had had a demeanour that was arrogantly remote—whereas she already knew that Markos possessed a latent sensuality capable of wrapping its tentacles about a woman's senses.

Even hers?

Perhaps…

But the fact that Markos Lyonedes now appeared every inch the powerful and arrogant Greek billionaire businessman that he was, instead of the flirtatiously seductive man of a few seconds ago, would seem to indicate that she had indeed overstepped the line. As far as he was concerned, at least.

Eva had only wanted to let him know that she had no intention of being so much as flattered by his marked attention, let alone falling for his seductive and no doubt practised—charm.

She gave a light and deliberately dismissive laugh. 'I'm only repeating what the gossips are saying about you.'

'Indeed?' That green gaze was hard and unyielding. 'And do you always listen to rumours rather than forming your own opinions of people?'

She shrugged. 'It's an unwise woman who ignores gossip completely.' Just as it was an unwise woman who chose to ignore the fact that Markos Lyonedes's voice had hardened in the last few minutes. Those clipped tones now betrayed the fact that English was not his native tongue.

'No doubt allowing you to decide that there is no smoke without fire...?'

Oh, Eva was pretty sure there was a *lot* of fire when this man chose to turn his lethal charm on a woman. 'Not exactly,' she dismissed dryly. 'There have been dozens of photographs of you with beautiful woman in the newspapers over the years. And articles in glossy magazines. Those things aside, I do have eyes and common sense with which to make up my own mind.'

His nostrils flared. 'And yet you had already decided to distrust me, from what you had heard of my reputation, before we had even met?'

Eva had decided so much more than that! 'I knew enough to be wary, yes.'

Markos Lyonedes's jaw tightened. 'You are not prepared to give me the benefit of the doubt?'

'In what way?'

'In that photographs in newspapers can often be deceiving, and gossip misleading.'

'Probably not, no,' she answered without hesitation.

'That's a pity.'

'Is it?'

His mouth tightened and he gave a stiff inclination of his head. 'I trust I did not interrupt your enjoyment of the evening?'

She grimaced. 'I wasn't enjoying it much even before you came over and spoke to me.'

'And my conversation has added to that lack of enjoyment?'

Eva shrugged. 'I shouldn't let it bother you, Markos; it's really nothing personal.'

'On the contrary. I believe your comments in regard to me to have been *very* personal,' he responded tersely.

Eva looked up at him, realising that although he appeared outwardly controlled, inwardly Markos Lyonedes was quietly, chillingly angry—as the tightness of his jaw and the angry glitter of those green eyes testified. Maybe playing this silly game of cat-and-mouse with him over this past week had not been a good move on her part.

She gave a dismissive shake of her head. 'I just thought I would save you wasting any of your time in attempting to charm me.'

'Would it be wasted?'

'Most definitely,' Eva confirmed with feeling.

His eyes became glacial. 'In that case, I will relieve you of the necessity of suffering my company a moment longer.'

Was that disappointment Eva now felt at this man's acceptance of her scathing dismissal of him? Surely it couldn't be—not when she knew from her cousin Donna how callous this man could be?

Donna should have known better than to become involved with a man like Markos Lyonedes in the first place, of course. But then, her cousin had never had the most discerning of tastes when it came to her choice in men—a family trait on the female side, if Eva's mother and Eva were any example. Having now met the man herself, Eva could perhaps better understand Donna's attraction to him. A fatal attraction and, in Eva's opinion, one that applied to *any* woman Markos Lyonedes became involved with. The man was far too powerful and attractive for his own good. He had only to click his fingers to have any woman he wanted.

Except Eva.

She and Donna had often stayed with their maternal grandparents when they were children, and during those visits they had developed a healthy competitiveness towards each other. A competitiveness which had become less healthy in adulthood, unfortunately, resulting in their rarely meeting as they pursued their separate careers and lifestyles, particularly once Eva had married Jack and moved to New York. But when Eva's marriage had finally come to an agonising end Donna had been the only one in her family to bother telephoning Eva to commiserate.

In fact her cousin had been ecstatic when she'd first called and told Eva of her relationship with Markos Lyonedes. She's been able to talk of nothing but how wonderful he was, and how much she longed to become his wife. When Markos Lyonedes had suddenly dumped Donna, just over a month ago, it had seemed only fair for Eva to listen sympathetically when her cousin called almost every day to talk endlessly of how much she was still in love with him.

Even if Eva hadn't been warned off by Donna's unhappy experience with Markos Lyonedes, she knew she would still have been wary of him. He was everything her broken marriage had taught her to stay well away from. Too rich. Too handsome. Far too powerful. And, as she now knew, too immediately and lethally sensual!

It was perhaps the latter trait that Eva found most disturbing. She knew that she wasn't as immune to that inborn sensuality, the way this man looked, or the hard leanness of his body, as she might have hoped or wished to be.

She had met dozens of handsome and charming

men during the three years since her separation and divorce—had even tried dating some of them. But not a single one of those men had touched her emotions, and nor had they dispelled the cynicism of feeling she now felt in regard to relationships.

Markos Lyonedes was such a forceful presence, even in a room full of equally powerful men—one of them was a US Senator, for goodness' sake!—that Eva had become aware of him the moment he had entered the room a short time ago. When he had looked at her a few minutes ago she had felt a shiver down the length of her spine as she'd recognised the admiration in his heated green gaze.

'I will leave you to enjoy the rest of your evening,' Eva finally replied derisively. 'I'm sure all the other ladies present will be only too happy to entertain you.'

Markos looked down at her piercingly. 'Is it possible the two of us have met before?'

Those amber eyes widened. 'Not that I'm aware, no.'

Not that Markos was aware, either—he was sure he would have remembered if he had ever met this voluptuously beautiful woman before. Even so, he sensed there was something more to Eva's comments regarding his reputation than her offhand dismissal implied. As far as he was aware, none of the women he had been involved with had ever walked away broken-hearted.

Or could it be that he was just too used to having women falling over themselves to attract his attention rather than the other way around? That he had believed Eva would feel flattered at his marked attention? If that was indeed the case then it was worse than arrogant of him, and he deservced the scorn she made no effort to hide.

Markos forced the tension from his shoulders. 'You—'

'Ah, there you are, Eva baby.' A tall, blond-haired man in his late thirties moved in beside Eva. His blue gaze was curious as he turned to smile at Markos, his teeth very white and straight against his slight tan. 'Great party, isn't it?'

'Great,' Markos echoed, as he inwardly acknowledged that he wasn't pleased at seeing the other man's arm draped possessively about Eva's waist. This was ridiculous of him, when Eva had made it so obvious that she had no interest in him. Perhaps the other man's proprietorial attitude explained that lack of interest?

Maybe. Although Eva hadn't looked particularly pleased at being called 'Eva baby'.

She straightened away from that possessive arm about her waist before making the introductions. 'Markos, this is Glen Asher. Glen, meet Markos Lyonedes.'

'Really? *The* Markos Lyonedes?' Glen prompted warmly as the two men shook hands.

'Yes, really,' Eva confirmed, irritated that Glen was so obviously bowled over by meeting him.

Admittedly the man was as rich as Croesus, but he was too handsome and charming for his own good. And Lyonedes Enterprises was one of the most powerful business organisations in the world, owning a private jet, as well as properties all over the world—including, Eva believed, their own private island in the Aegean. But did Glen *have* to look quite so impressed?

'Lyonedes Tower is a monument to beautiful architecture,' Glen added admiringly.

In that, Eva did have to agree with him. Standing

at least eighty floors high, and built of a pale, rose-coloured marble, with tinted sun-reflecting windows, Lyonedes Tower was one of the most beautiful buildings in New York, rivalling the Empire State and the Chrysler Buildings.

Even so...

'It's just another tall building blocking the view, Glen,' she dismissed impatiently.

Markos Lyonedes looked amused rather than annoyed by her comment. 'But I thank you anyway,' he told the other man dryly.

Eva's irritation deepened. 'I believe it's time we were leaving, Glen.'

He looked crestfallen. 'But we only just got here...'

Markos's previous annoyance at Eva's scathing comments about his reputation had dissipated totally in the face of her increasing irritation with the man who had accompanied her here this evening. If she *was* in a serious relationship, it wasn't with Glen Asher, and Markos couldn't see how a man Eva was involved with would be happy about her attending a party with another man—particularly one as handsome and obviously successful as Glen.

So, no serious relationship.

But what did it matter? The woman he knew only as 'Just Eva' couldn't have made her complete lack of interest in him any more obvious. Contrarily, it just made her all the more intriguing to Markos.

He had never thought of himself as being a masochist before, but maybe this move to New York, and the over-abundance of beautiful women vying for his attention this past week, was turning him into one—because if anything his attraction to Eva had only deepened in the last few minutes.

He looked down at her from between hooded lids. 'I would be more than happy to escort Eva to her home if you would like to remain at the party a while longer, Glen.'

Amber-gold eyes widened in what looked like horror at the suggestion, even as bright spots of colour brightened those pale alabaster cheeks. 'If Glen wishes to stay, I'm perfectly capable of ordering a cab and taking myself home, thank you,' she replied tightly.

He continued to look down at her. 'There's no need when my car is parked downstairs.'

Eva wanted to tell Markos Lyonedes what he could do with his car!

But, even more important than that, she now deeply regretted having invited Glen to accompany her here this evening in the first place.

They had met the previous week, at a party similar to this one. Eva had studied him dispassionately, finding that she approved of his blond hair and blue eyes, and the fact that he was tall and appeared healthy.

On the basis that she couldn't just march up to a complete stranger and ask him to be the donor for her IVF baby—once tests had proved he was fertile, of course—Eva had decided it might be better if the two of them got to know each other a little better before she dropped the bombshell on Glen. That was the only reason she had gone to his office early yesterday evening and asked him to be her escort to Senator Ashcroft's cocktail party tonight.

Although Glen seemed to have a very different idea of where their relationship was going...

She gave Markos Lyonedes a brightly insincere smile. 'It's very kind of you to offer, Markos, but—'

'But there's absolutely no need when I'm happy to leave with Eva,' Glen cut in with smooth confidence, his arm once again moving about Eva's waist. 'I booked dinner for the two of us at nine-thirty,' he added temptingly.

A dinner that he was no doubt hoping would result in the two of them sharing the bed in his apartment later on this evening, or possibly in Eva's. But Eva knew that sharing Glen's bed—or any other man's, come to that—simply wasn't going to happen.

Nor, in this day and age, was it necessary. It had all seemed perfectly logical when Eva had made her decision several months ago. She was desperate to have a child of her own, but not another marriage or relationship with a man who would ultimately let her down. One failed marriage was surely enough for any woman.

She had it all planned out. She would become pregnant before her thirtieth birthday in six months' time, move her offices to her apartment and continue working from there until her eighth month, have the baby, and then resume working once the baby was three months old or so, hiring a nanny who could take over on the occasions Eva had to go out and visit with her clients.

Logic. Not emotion.

Except it wasn't logic which drove Eva but an aching, driving need. Jack had wanted to try for a baby as soon as they were married, and as a family of her own was what Eva wanted too she had been only too happy to agree to the suggestion. Month after month she had waited to see if *this* was going to be the month when she could excitedly tell Jack she was pregnant. Except it hadn't happened. Not the first year. Nor the second. Until in the end they had decided to see a specialist and find out if either of them had a problem—and, if they did, what to do about it.

The results of those tests had been devastating and, although Eva hadn't realised it at the time, they had also sounded the death knell to her marriage.

Jack was sterile. One hundred per cent, no room for error, sterile.

Oh, they had told each other that it didn't matter, that they had each other. It had only been when Eva suggested that maybe they could adopt that the chasm had widened even further between them. Jack had adamantly refused to consider adoption, stating that his blue-blood New York family would never accept as heir a child who wasn't biologically Jack's.

Eva had tried to believe that having each other really *was* enough. While each day she had died a little inside at the knowledge that there would never be any children in her marriage. No babies to love and nurture, her own or adopted. No happy house full of the children, she had longed for all her life after growing up an only child in the war zone that had been her parents' marriage.

She and Jack had stayed together for another two years after the specialist had delivered his devastating news. Years during which they had drifted apart as they both buried themselves in their individual careers rather than face the ever-widening rift in their marriage. Years when Jack became involved in affair after affair—possibly as a sop to his dented virility?—only to break them off each time Eva found out about them, with tears and declarations of love on his part, and promises of future fidelity. Until the next time. And the next.

Eva's love for Jack had died a little more with each of those affairs. Until there had been nothing left but the shell of their marriage. A marriage Eva wouldn't have wanted to bring a child into even if it had been possible.

Another three years of being on her own after the divorce, of building her interior design business into one of the most successful in New York, and Eva had realised there was still something missing from her life. The same something that had always been missing from her life.

A baby of her own.

Lots of professional women had babies on their own nowadays—so why not Eva? She certainly had enough money to be able to provide for them both comfortably, and her career was of a kind that could be worked around a baby's needs.

So the plan was to find herself a man who was healthy, explain to him what it meant to be an IVF donor, and present him with the legal contract she would expect him to sign. Both of them would be protected from any financial demands being made on the other after the baby was born.

Putting that idea into practice had proved much harder than Eva had imagined. Broaching the subject, asking any man to coldly, clinically donate his sperm for IVF, had proved difficult.

'That's very thoughtful of you, Glen.' She smiled warmly, more for Markos Lyonedes's benefit than Glen's. Her smile faded as she turned to look at the Greek businessman. 'If you will excuse us?'

'Of course.' Markos gave a slight inclination of his head, wondering what thoughts had been going through Eva's head these past few minutes to form that frown between those golden eyes. Whatever they had been, he certainly didn't hold out a lot of hope for Glen Asher's chances of sharing her bed tonight. 'It was a pleasure to meet you both.'

'And you,' Glen assured him warmly.

It was a warmth that was in no way reflected in Eva's incredible gold eyes, and she made no effort to echo her escort's enthusiasm. 'We'll wish you a good evening, then, Mr Lyonedes.'

His eyes laughed down into hers. 'I believe you called me Markos earlier.'

'Did I?' she dismissed coolly. 'How over-familiar of me!'

Not familiar enough for Markos. He turned to watch Eva and her escort cross the room to make their excuses to their host before leaving. All without those amber-gold eyes giving so much as a glance back in his direction.

Markos continued to watch the sensuous sway of those curvaceous hips so lovingly outlined in that clinging red gown, and made a silent promise to himself as the doorman closed the door behind Eva's departure.

A promise that one day—or night; it didn't really matter what time it was!—he would hear Eva scream his name as he made love to her.

CHAPTER THREE

'WELL, well, well—if it isn't Ms Evangeline Grey come to call at last!' Markos observed dryly from where he sat in his high-backed leather chair behind the mahogany desk in his office.

Lena had shown the interior designer in at exactly five o'clock on Monday evening, before quietly closing the door behind her as she left them alone together.

Markos and the interior designer Evangeline Grey.

The same Evangeline Grey who had introduced herself to him as 'Just Eva' on Saturday evening, in the knowledge that she had cancelled two appointments with him earlier in the week.

Markos had wasted no time after she and Glen had left the party on Saturday in asking one of Senator Ashcroft's many aides about the identity of the woman in the red dress. Only to be informed that she was the interior designer Evangeline Grey.

Those amber-gold eyes flashed her displeasure now, as she marched into the centre of the spacious office, allowing Markos to see that she managed to look sexy even wearing a business suit—a fitted black jacket and knee-length black skirt, the latter revealing long and silky-smooth legs. Her silk blouse was the same unusual colour as her eyes; her long ebony hair neatly gathered and secured at her crown.

'Your telephone call this morning made it clear you expected me to be here promptly at five o'clock, whether it was convenient or otherwise,' she reminded him with barely concealed impatience.

'Indeed.' Markos stood up and moved slowly round his desk to lean back against it as he looked down at her between narrowed lids. 'And the fact that you are here would seem to imply that you were no happier than I was on Saturday at the possibility of having a slur cast upon your reputation?'

A frown appeared on that smooth alabaster brow. 'That's hardly a fair comparison, Mr Lyonedes, when the threats you made to me this morning were in regard to my professional reputation, not my personal one.'

'I believe the saying is "payback can be a bitch"?' He gave an unrepentant shrug. This woman had wilfully—deliberately!—played with him on Saturday evening by not revealing her true identity, and no doubt been highly amused at Markos's expense because of it.

Markos had thought about it long and hard over the weekend, finally deciding that if Evangeline Grey wanted to play games then he was happy to oblige her. With that in mind he had telephoned her office himself that morning and demanded to speak to her personally. After a short delay there had been a more or less one-sided conversation during which Markos had informed her that there would be no more cancelled appointments. If she didn't want him to tell anyone and everyone who cared to listen just how unreliable he had found her professional services she would come at five.

Her only answer had been to end the call abruptly,

causing Markos to chuckle wryly as he slowly placed his mobile down on his desktop.

Nevertheless, he had been sure that Eva *would* be here at five o'clock. He knew that she was now aware that it was well within his power to seriously damage her professional reputation if he chose to do so.

'You're unusually quiet today,' he remarked, lifting his dark brows mockingly.

Oh, Eva had plenty she wanted to say to this man. She was just erring on the side of caution—for the moment.

She had realised after leaving Senator Ashcroft's cocktail party on Saturday—her feelings of anger on behalf of her cousin aside—that it probably hadn't been a wise move on her part to antagonise a man as powerful as Markos Lyonedes by making appointments with him which she'd never had any intention of keeping. Unwise and not a little childish, she now accepted reproachfully. As if it would *really* matter to a man as powerful as Markos Lyonedes if some little interior designer chose to snub him by not keeping her appointments!

Except, having met her on Saturday evening, it obviously *did* matter to him. It didn't help, having duly arrived at Lyonedes Tower at five o'clock, that Eva was now totally aware of the way in which Markos Lyonedes managed to exude a predatory air—despite the expensive elegance of his tailored dark grey suit and paler grey silk shirt, with matching tie knotted meticulously at his throat.

'Did you and Glen enjoy your late dinner on Saturday evening?' he prompted softly.

Eva's mouth tightened at this reminder of the time

she and Glen had spent together at an Italian restaurant after leaving the Senator's party. Several hours during which she had desperately tried to dredge up some of her former approval of Glen as an IVF donor, only to find that, rather than appreciating Glen's healthy good looks, she was comparing them to the hard and chiselled features of the man now standing in front of her.

A man she wouldn't even *consider* putting on a shortlist of potential donors for her baby.

Oh, Markos Lyonedes was definitely handsome, and obviously he was healthy and intelligent, but there all suitability as the possible father of her child ended. Markos might have more than earned his reputation for avoiding serious relationships, but Eva knew there was no way that a man as powerful as one of the Greek Lyonedes cousins would ever agree to clinically, calculatedly father a child by donating his sperm for IVF.

In fact her experience with Glen now made her wonder if it might not be better to opt for an anonymous donor after all. In the meantime, she had to cope with knowing she was physically responsive to Markos in a way she hadn't experienced in the three years since her divorce—if ever!

Jack had been several years older than her when they'd married, and more experienced. Their lovemaking had been fun to explore at the start of their marriage. That interest, for obvious reasons, had eventually faded. To the point that by the end of their marriage, they hadn't made love in months.

Eva's self-esteem had been at a very low ebb after the divorce, her confidence in her desirability even lower, and it had taken months for her even to go out on a date with another man—only to discover that her emotions were completely numb, and the most she could feel for any of those men was a distant liking.

But it wasn't anything as lukewarm as *liking*— distant or otherwise!—she felt in regard to Markos Lyonedes.

Eva had been convinced—with the experience of her disastrous marriage behind her, and after listening for hours to Donna's broken-hearted meanderings down the telephone as her cousin mourned her lost love—that she was destined to be the one woman who wouldn't *ever* be stupid enough to fall under the sensual spell of all that lethal Lyonedes charm and charismatic good-looks.

Which only went to prove what an arrogant fool she had been.

Because Eva now knew she only had to be in the same room as Markos Lyonedes to be aware of every single thing about him. She could feel the tug of that desire even now, causing her hands to tremble slightly, her breasts to feel hot and swollen, and a dampness between her thighs.

She could see the same desire reflected towards her in the warmth of those dark green eyes. It was a physical attunement that seemed to make the very air between them crackle and dance.

'It was fine,' Eva dismissed abruptly. 'Now, if we could—'

'Have you and Glen been together long?'

Eva frowned slightly. 'I'm not sure that it's any of your business, but we haven't "been together" at all.'

Eva had gently but firmly refused Glen's suggestion, before they parted on Saturday evening, that the two of them might go out together again this week, having lost all interest in him with regard to approaching him about IVF.

Markos raised questioning brows. 'Yet…?'

'Really, Mr Lyonedes—'

'Markos.'

'Markos.' She gave a brief, meaningless smile of acknowledgement. 'I really didn't come here to discuss my personal life—so if we could we just get down to business?'

Markos settled more comfortably against the front of the desk and folded his arms across his chest. He considered Eva with narrowed but appreciative eyes. Her features really were extremely delicate: those gold-coloured eyes, high cheekbones, slender jaw, those full and sensuous lips glossed a deep peach today. With her hair secured at her crown it was now possible to see the slender arch of Eva's delicious throat, with skin as delicate as pale china.

It was a delectable delicacy that Markos found himself aching to taste. Presumably that wasn't completely out of the question, if Eva and Glen really weren't together.

He straightened slowly. 'That's a pity, because the only thing that I'm in the least interested in talking about this evening *is* your personal life.'

Those gold eyes widened warily. 'I don't understand.'

'No?'

Markos found himself watching intently as she moistened those peach-glossed lips before speaking again.

'I understood from our telephone conversation earlier today that you wanted me here at five o'clock so that we could discuss possible new designs for the décor in your apartment.'

Markos smiled slightly. 'I don't remember so much as mentioning any designs for my apartment during our brief conversation this morning.'

'Well…no,' she conceded slowly, after a few seconds' thought. 'But that was the reason for our two earlier appointments.'

'Two appointments which you didn't ever have any intention of keeping.'

'No.'

'Why not?'

Eva felt about two inches tall as she realised she had behaved like an idiot. But it had just been so tempting, when she had received the call the previous week from Markos Lyonedes's secretary, asking if she would come to his office to discuss the possibility of redesigning the interior of his apartment. Tempting to accept and then cancel as a small way of showing him that not *every* woman jumped at the click of his fingers.

She should have realised—given more consideration to the repercussions of her behaviour if the powerful Markos Lyonedes decided to make an issue of it.

Her gaze didn't quite meet his now. 'I really did have to be somewhere else on Monday evening.'

'And Friday?' He quirked dark brows. 'Did you really have an emergency appointment with your dentist?'

'Er—yes.'

Markos eyed her warily. 'Would you care to explain?'

She grimaced. 'Perhaps when I introduced the two

of you on Saturday evening I should have mentioned that Glen *is* a dentist.'

His mouth thinned. 'I see.'

She winced. 'Do you…?'

'Oh, I think so.' Markos nodded slowly, his interest well and truly piqued by the woman now standing in front of him. More than piqued, if he were honest. Markos had no idea why it should be, but he found everything about Eva Grey intriguing. From her lippy conversation to her desirable hourglass figure. 'You obviously felt an urgent need to have a cavity filled.'

Those golden eyes widened in blank shock, her cheeks filling with colour as she gasped her indignation.

Now it was Markos's turn to chuckle at Eva's expense. And for that chuckle to develop into full-throated laughter as he saw that he really had succeeded in rendering this complicated woman speechless. 'My God, Eva, you should see your face!' he finally managed through his laughter. 'Or maybe not; you look a little like a fish out of water at the moment.'

Probably because Eva *felt* like a fish out of water at that moment. Mouth opening and shutting, her chest rapidly rising and falling as she gasped for breath, her eyes wide and staring. 'I can't believe you just said that!'

'Actually, neither can I.' He sobered. 'My Aunt Karelia would consider my conversation most ungentlemanly. Unfortunately for you, I'm more than happy to risk her disapproval if I've succeeded in rendering you speechless for once!'

'Really?'

'Really,' Markos confirmed teasingly, aware that

Eva was still having trouble regaining her usual spiky confidence.

She gave a disbelieving shake of her head. 'Your Aunt Karelia would be perfectly correct in her assessment of your behaviour just now.'

'She usually is,' he acknowledged ruefully.

A frown appeared between those golden eyes. 'Who is your Aunt Karelia, exactly? And why does her opinion matter to you?'

Markos gave an affectionate smile. 'My cousin Drakon's mother. She's also been a mother to me since I was eight years old—after I went to live with her and my Uncle Theo when my parents were killed in a plane crash.'

Eva drew her breath in sharply as she heard the pain underlying the practicality of Markos's tone. She hadn't known that about him—hadn't cared to know that about him—and she frowned slightly as she acknowledged that his confiding that information to her had introduced a different sort of intimacy between the two of them from their previous physical awareness, which had seemed to sizzle and crackle in the air only minutes ago. An intimacy that was emotional rather than physical.

'I'm sorry for your loss,' she murmured finally.

'Thank you,' he accepted gruffly.

Eva shifted uncomfortably. 'Did you like living with your cousin and his parents?'

His grin warmed his eyes to the colour of emeralds. 'Eventually. I was pretty traumatised the first year or so, and probably gave my Aunt Karelia a few grey hairs. But eventually I settled down, and I really couldn't have asked for a better surrogate family.'

'You and Drakon are close?'

'As brothers,' he confirmed without hesitation.

Eva raised dark brows. 'I met him a couple of times when he was in New York. I didn't find him a particularly warm man.' Tall, dark and gorgeous, yes—just like his cousin Markos—but there was a single-minded ruthlessness to Drakon Lyonedes that he made no effort to hide.

Was it a trait his cousin also possessed…?

Probably, Eva concluded, remembering how Markos had changed on Saturday evening, his manner going from lazily charming to coolly precise, after she had made the comment concerning how he ended his relationships. In fact, apart from the heat of desire that glinted in Markos's eyes when he looked at her—something that had certainly never been present on the two occasions when Eva had met the coldly remote Drakon Lyonedes—the cousins were very much alike: heart-stoppingly gorgeous and lethally powerful.

Markos's grin widened. 'That's probably because you aren't a blonde with sea-blue eyes named Gemini!'

'Gemini is your cousin's new wife?'

'It's been very much a case of "how the mighty are fallen"!' Markos nodded. 'One look at Gemini and Drakon was knocked off his feet.'

'I somehow can't imagine *anything* knocking your cousin off his feet.' Eva eyed him disbelievingly.

Markos shrugged. 'Neither could I until it happened.'

This conversation had become altogether too personal for Eva's liking. 'Interesting as this conversation is, it's getting late, Markos,' she said briskly.

He raised those dark brows. 'Do you have yet another appointment to go to this evening?'

She could so easily have said yes. But instead… 'Well…no. But—'

'But what?'

'But it's Monday evening, and I always clean my apartment on Monday evenings,' Eva rallied weakly.

He eyed her mockingly. 'I thought that was what the weekends were for?'

She gave a disbelieving snort. 'Admit it, Markos, you've never had to clean your own apartment, or anywhere else you've lived, at the weekends or any other time!'

'Not true. I had to keep my own rooms clean when I was at university in Oxford.' He grimaced. 'Admittedly I couldn't see the bedroom carpet for the clutter after the first few weeks, and I ran out of clean clothes on a regular basis, but I coped.'

'By ignoring the clutter and buying new clothes, probably,' she guessed derisively.

'Guilty as charged,' Markos admitted with an unrepentant grin.

'That is so— Oh, *wow*…!' Eva gasped as she noticed the view from the huge picture window behind him for the first time—surely testament to exactly how powerfully attractive she found Markos, because the view from the window was amazing. New York City in all its glory.

Eva continued to look at the New York skyline as she slowly walked over to the window, dazzled by the combination of the tall, gleaming buildings and the lush green park.

'I seem to recall you said you thought of Lyonedes Tower as just another tall building blocking the view,' Markos reminded her as he joined her at the window.

Eva gave a wince at this reminder of the bluntness of her conversation when they first met. 'I may have been a little…impolite to you at the party on Saturday evening.'

'May have been?' he taunted softly.

'I *was* impolite,' she conceded.

'Any particular reason why…?'

'Does there have to be a reason?' Eva glanced sideways at Markos, totally aware of how close he was now standing to her. Close enough for her to inhale the heady combination of the lemon soap and sandalwood aftershave. Close enough that their arms were almost touching. Close enough that Eva was now fully aware of the heat emanating from Markos's body.

Close enough that Eva could barely breathe for wanting to close that short distance between them and lose herself to the feel of those sensuously chiselled lips devouring her own.

Instead she rushed into speech. 'I behaved badly—unprofessionally—and I apologise.'

He arched dark brows. 'Does that mean you've reconsidered and are now willing to give me—and my reputation—the benefit of the doubt…?'

'I'm not sure I would go that far,' she said warily.

'Liar,' Markos murmured huskily. He'd seen the way those luscious golden eyes had darkened to amber, the slight flush appearing in Eva's porcelain cheeks. Her lips were slightly moist and parted. As if waiting to be kissed.

As if she realised that was Markos's intention, Eva took a step back and away from him. 'I really do have to go now. If you've changed your mind about considering my designs—' She broke off as Markos took another step forward, until they were now once again standing so close they were almost touching. She gave a determined shake of her head. 'Markos, if you're trying to intimidate me then I think I should warn you—'

'Warn me of what...?' Markos murmured throatily, even as he raised one of his hands to cup the warmth of her cheek, before moving the soft pad of his thumb over the softness of her lips, feeling the warmth of her breath against his fingers as he parted those lips in preparation for his kiss.

His own arousal intensified at the feel of that sensual warmth against his skin. His shaft was hard and pulsing, demanding...

Eva's eyes were wide, deep amber pools as she stared up at him. 'I should warn you—'

'Yes...?' Markos prompted softly, holding that wide and startled gaze with his own as his head began to lower towards hers.

She breathed softly. 'I really should warn you—'

'Warn me later, hmm?' he dismissed gruffly, before finally claiming those full and pouting lips with his own.

Eva totally forgot what it was she wanted to warn Markos about as his other arm moved firmly about her waist and he pulled her in tightly against the heat of his body, angling her face up to his before his mouth finally took possession of hers.

Markos's kiss was everything that Eva had known it would be—not in any way a gentle exploration, but an instant explosion of the senses, taste, smell, feel, and it felt so good to be against the hard heat of his body as they kissed hungrily, deeply, lips devouring, tongues duelling.

Eva tightly gripped Markos's shoulders, her legs feeling weak as he crushed the ache of her breasts against his chest. Heat pooled between her thighs as she felt the hard throb of his arousal pressing insistently against her.

The sky could have fallen at that moment, the building collapsed around them, and Eva wouldn't have noticed, too lost in the heat that consumed them both as Markos's hands moved down to cup her bottom and pull her in more tightly. He ground his erection against and into her even as their mouths drank greedily of each other.

Eva was on fire, her inner ice melting, and her fingers became entangled in the dark hair at Markos's nape as she returned that heat, needing, wanting—

She *wanted* Markos Lyonedes…!

CHAPTER FOUR

'Oн, I'm terribly sorry! I had no idea…!'

Eva wrenched her mouth free of Markos's to push against the hardness of his chest in an effort to free herself as she heard that startled gasp from the other side of the room. Her cheeks were aflame with embarrassed colour as she turned to see the middle-aged woman who had shown her into the office earlier—obviously Markos's secretary—now standing in the open doorway, her eyes wide with shock at having interrupted them in a moment of intimacy.

Eva's efforts to free herself proved totally ineffective as Markos's arms tightened about her. 'Let go of me!' she said fiercely under her breath.

His only answer was to give her an amused glance before turning to look at the woman still standing in the doorway. 'Are you ready to leave for the day…?'

The woman looked flustered. 'I was about to, yes. I— Yes.'

In stark contrast, Markos appeared completely at his ease as he nodded. 'Thanks, Lena, I'll see you in the morning.'

'Mr Lyonedes. Ms Grey.' The woman Markos called Lena didn't meet either of their gazes before she quickly turned and left the room, closing the door briskly behind her.

'I asked you to let go of me!' Eva instructed, agitated as she once again pushed against the solid muscle that was Markos's chest. That particular moment of madness was definitely over.

'Do I have to?'

'Yes!'

'Why?'

Eva glared up at him. 'Because I asked you to.'

He regarded her with amused green eyes. 'And do you always get what you ask for?'

Sometimes Eva got a lot more than she asked for! For instance, she hadn't asked to be attracted to this man. Just as she hadn't asked to enjoy his experienced lips moving so surely and sensually against and over her own. Or to feel her heart almost leap out of her chest as she recognised her own desire to feel and taste the hardness of Markos's obvious arousal throbbing against the heat of her thighs. All of them were emotions Eva had believed herself to be incapable of feeling. Emotions she didn't *want* to feel!

Her eyes narrowed. 'Don't say I didn't warn you…' she murmured, before reaching behind her to grasp one of his hands, bringing it forward before bending the wrist up at a painful angle as she slipped deftly out of his arms before releasing him.

'Ouch!' Markos frowned as he grasped his pained wrist. 'Where did you learn to do that?' He eyed her with bemusement once he was sure nothing was broken.

'Self-defence classes.' She briskly straightened her jacket before checking that her hair was still neatly secured at her nape, sincerely hoping that Markos couldn't see that her hands were trembling as she did so. 'A necessary evil since I moved to New York.' She shrugged unapologetically.

'Hmm.' Markos grimaced as he once again leant back against his desk. 'You never did tell me the reason you moved to New York.'

She raised dark brows. 'Probably because that's another one of those things I consider personal.'

Markos regarded her from between narrowed lids for several long seconds. 'There was obviously a man involved,' he finally murmured speculatively.

She gave a derisive laugh. 'What a typically arrogant male conclusion.'

He shrugged broad shoulders, unconcerned. 'That's probably because I *am* a typically arrogant male.'

'And obviously proud of it,' she scorned.

Markos wouldn't say he was proud of it. It was just the way it was. His father and uncle had founded Lyonedes Enterprises before he was even born, and he and Drakon had added considerably to the success of the company's businesses worldwide since taking over completely when his Uncle Theo died ten years ago. There would be little point in Markos denying that this success, and the power that came along with it, had resulted in a certain assured arrogance in both himself and Drakon.

He grimaced unapologetically. 'It is what it is. And you, Ms Evangeline Grey, are deliberately trying to change the subject from my original question,' he added knowingly.

Yes, she was. Because Eva was uncomfortably aware she didn't want to answer Markos's original question.

Divorce, the ultimate admission of the failure of a marriage, was something that not even Eva's parents had succumbed to—even if they should have done so years ago, rather than slowly destroying each other with the bitterness of their disappointment. Eva wasn't in the least proud of her failed marriage, and nor did she wish to talk about it.

Her chin rose determinedly before she turned Markos's earlier comment back on him. 'It is what it is.'

Which told Markos precisely nothing. 'I can easily make the necessary enquiries that would give me the answer to that question…'

Her mouth tightened. 'That's your prerogative.'

'But I won't,' Markos concluded dryly. 'I would so much rather wait for you to tell me about yourself than listen to inaccurate gossip,' he added, in answer to her questioning look.

Her face flushed. 'If that was a dig at me for the things I said to you on Saturday—'

'It wasn't,' he assured her softly. 'I would just rather wait for you to confide in me.'

She gave a dismissive snort. 'Then you'll be waiting a long time.'

Patience had never particularly been a part of Markos's character, but he had a feeling that where this intriguing woman was concerned it might well be worth the wait…

'I have no plans to leave New York for the foreseeable future, Eva,' he said huskily.

Eva was well aware of that—which was why, after the mess she had made of things with this man, she was seriously considering relocating her office to

Outer Mongolia, or possibly Antarctica—anywhere but New York!

Because this second meeting with Markos Lyonedes had shown her that he wasn't at all what she had assumed he was after listening to Donna bemoan how callously he had brought an end to their relationship. He was arrogant, yes, but it wasn't the over-bloated self-aggrandizement Eva had expected to find—more an inborn confidence in who and what he was. Markos had demonstrated that he was capable of dealing with, and returning, any challenge she might care to give him. He also had a wicked sense of humour, which he was just as likely to turn on himself as he was anyone else. There was something very appealing about a man who could laugh at himself.

And Eva defied any woman to remain unaffected by that heady combination of charming self-assurance and devastating good-looks.

That brief and thankfully interrupted kiss they had shared had certainly proved to Eva that *she* wasn't immune to anything about Markos Lyonedes.

A man whose wealth and charm was everything and more than Jack, her ex-husband, had been...

Which was more than enough reason for Eva to take herself out of Markos's insidiously seductive company. *Right now!*

'Then I hope you enjoy the city,' she told him lightly. 'Now, if you will excuse me...'

'Haven't you forgotten something?'

Eva paused before turning back reluctantly to answer that softly spoken query. 'Have I?'

He gave a mocking inclination of his head. 'You haven't been up to look at my apartment yet.'

She tensed warily. 'Up...?'

Markos gave a husky chuckle even as he glanced pointedly towards the ceiling above them. 'Up.'

Markos's apartment was on the floor above this one? All this time there had been a bedroom—probably several—right above them? Oh, good Lord...!

Eva drew in a deep breath before speaking. 'I think you're right. It really wouldn't be a good idea for me to work for you—'

'Coward.'

'I beg your pardon?' she gasped softly.

Once again he shrugged those broad shoulders. 'I called you a coward.'

'Because I don't want to work for you?' She eyed him incredulously.

Markos shook his head slowly. 'Because we both know the reason you don't want to work for me.'

Her jaw tightened. 'Which is?'

'You're afraid.'

'You think I'm *afraid* of you?' she said disbelievingly.

'I think that you're afraid of how you feel when you're with me,' Markos corrected softly. 'You're more comfortable in the company of a man like Glen Asher because you know you can manipulate and control him in a way you would never be able to do with me.'

All the colour drained from Eva's cheeks. She knew that every word Markos spoke was the truth. Oh, not about Glen. But she *was* frightened—of Markos, and of what he made her feel when she was with him.

She didn't want to feel that way about any man. After her divorce she had been relieved to feel so numb, to know that she would never again have to go through the pain of a broken relationship.

To now realise that Markos Lyonedes had penetrated her emotions, if only on a physical level, was *not* a welcome revelation.

'Has anyone ever told you that you have an ego the size of Manhattan?' She snorted disgustedly.

'Not that I recall, no.' He gave a slow and confident smile. 'Was anything I said to you just now untrue?'

Her mouth thinned. 'I'm not afraid of you.'

'Then why not prove it by agreeing to redesign the interior of my apartment?'

Eva gave a disbelieving shake of her head. 'I'm twenty-nine, Markos, not nine, and as such I'm not about to be goaded into a juvenile game of dare with you. Especially when I don't think it's a good idea for me to accept a commission from you.'

'Kirsty is going to be *so* disappointed about that,' he murmured regretfully.

'Kirsty?' she repeated warily.

'Kirsty Foster. Her husband, Gerry, is my PA, and she was the one who recommended your work to me,' he added pleasantly.

Ordinarily Eva would have been pleased to have her work so appreciated by one of her previous clients that they had chosen to recommend her to their friends. And she liked Kirsty Foster. The two women had remained friends even after Eva had completed the work on Kirsty's bedroom, often meeting for coffee and a chat. Not so much recently, Eva recalled guiltily, as the other woman's blossoming pregnancy was a painful reminder of her own aching hunger for a baby.

But Kirsty was the one who had recommended her

work to Markos Lyonedes. The same Markos Lyonedes who employed Kirsty's husband, Gerry...

Eva's eyes narrowed. 'Are you threatening me, Markos...?'

He eyed her innocently. 'I was merely commenting that Kirsty's husband works for me.'

'Which sounds suspiciously like a threat to me!'

His lips twitched with repressed humour. 'That's *your* prerogative, of course.'

Eva didn't know whether to admire him for his audacity or lambast him for his arrogance. Either way, she couldn't work for a man she didn't even like...

Lying to herself wasn't going to make this situation any easier, Eva immediately chastised herself. The problem was not that she didn't like Markos Lyonedes, but that a single kiss had shown her that physically she liked him too much. Eva had been convinced she would never—*could* never—feel again. She was determined not to feel physical desire for any man when she knew it would ultimately lead to more pain and disillusionment.

'What are you thinking about...?' Markos had watched Eva's expressions during the last few minutes of silence between them.

Had seen the dismay. The confusion. Followed by the doubt. And then what had looked like pained anguish. All of them emotions he would never previously have associated with the prickly and confident Eva.

She shook herself out of that mood of despondency with obvious effort. 'I was just... Obviously if Kirsty recommended me—perhaps we could reschedule another meeting for later in the week?' She gave a tight smile as she saw his sceptical expression. 'I promise not to cancel this time.'

Markos regarded her through narrowed lids. 'You never did say what the emergency was last Monday.'

Her smile turned to a look of exasperation. 'A client was having hysterics when the curtain material I had ordered, which I duly took round for her to approve before the curtains were made up, turned out *not* to be exactly the same colour as her husband's eyes after all.'

Markos's eyes widened. 'People really do things like that?'

She laughed softly. 'You would be surprised. I had a client a couple of years ago who matched the colour of her carpet to her Golden Labrador.'

'Must have made it difficult to find him when it came time to go for a walk!' Markos murmured—only to watch in satisfaction as Eva's laughter deepened, causing her eyes to glow a deep gold. 'Have dinner with me tomorrow evening,' he prompted abruptly.

'To discuss the changes you'd like in your apartment?'

'To discuss any damn thing you please.'

'I was trying to tell you earlier...' Eva frowned. 'I make a point of never mixing my professional life with my personal one.'

'So it's one or the other?'

Eva instantly added stubborn determination to the list of things she was rapidly discovering about Markos Lyonedes. 'I believe I've already taken you on as a client by agreeing to look at your apartment.'

'And if I would prefer to have dinner with you tomorrow evening instead?'

Eva's breath caught in her throat as her eyes widened. 'Would you...?'

He frowned darkly. 'Why don't we compromise and

make our next appointment in my apartment tomorrow evening at seven-thirty? That way I can arrange for us to have dinner together immediately afterwards, so that we can discuss any suggestions you might have.'

Manipulative determination. Eva wryly corrected that earlier addition to her ever-growing list of Markos's character attributes. 'I'm starting to see how you gave your Aunt Karelia grey hair!'

Markos gave a grin. 'Does that mean you accept my invitation?'

Did it? There were so many reasons why Eva shouldn't have dinner with Markos tomorrow evening—this man's callous treatment of her cousin being only one of them. But—and she inwardly apologised to Donna— that certainly wasn't the *main* reason Eva would prefer not to have dinner with Markos—tomorrow evening or any other time.

She straightened briskly. 'I don't think so, but thank you for asking.'

Markos eyed her frustratedly, knowing it wasn't just the desire to have Eva in his bed that made him so determined. He also enjoyed her company. He appreciated the spirited way she stood up to him. The way her dry sense of humour was more than a match for his own. And he couldn't help feeling curious as to what Eva had been thinking about earlier when she'd looked so wistful.

He raised dark brows. 'And if I intend to keep on asking…?'

She shrugged. 'Then I'll just have to keep on refusing.'

'And if I manage to wear you down…?'

'You won't.' She smiled.

'You sound very sure,' Markos said knowingly.

'I am.' She nodded.

Had any woman turned him down so emphatically before? Markos wondered with a frown. Not that he could ever remember, no. And, again, that wasn't arrogance talking—it was just a fact. Nor did he believe it was only Eva's reluctance to see him again that made her so attractive to him.

Everything about Eva intrigued him. Even her obvious boredom on Saturday evening with the other guests at the cocktail party—including him—as if she had attended one too many parties just like it and met one too many arrogant men to be impressed by yet another one.

That behaviour had been completely nullified by her heated response to him a few minutes ago—before she had shut down that response with the finality of a steel trapdoor closing about her emotions.

And what had seemed like an expression of sadness, even anguish, only added to the mystery and contradiction that was fast becoming Evangeline Grey.

Markos sensed Eva had secrets hidden behind those beautiful golden eyes. Several of them. Secrets he was longing for Eva to share with him.

'Okay.' He straightened to move and check the diary on his desktop. 'I'm busy tomorrow and Wednesday, but six o'clock on Thursday evening looks good.' He looked up at her enquiringly, wondering if it was wishful thinking on his part or if that really was a look of disappointment on her face because he was seeming to back off.

And he was only seeming to back off. Markos had no intention of giving up where Eva was concerned.

'Thursday at six is fine with me too,' Eva accepted abruptly, pretty sure that if she designed a colour scheme of pink and white, and ultra-feminine, it would ensure that Markos no longer wished to employ her. It would do absolutely nothing for her professional reputation, of course, but it might be worth it just to see the look on Markos's face when she presented the sketches to him!

'I'm learning to be wary of that particular look of amusement...' He eyed her suspiciously as he straightened.

Eva laughed softly. 'Just a private joke.'

'Design-wise, you should know that a harem theme or an explosion of pink ruffles is definitely out,' he commented dryly.

How had he guessed what she was thinking? 'Now you're ruining all my fun!'

'When I would so love to be the cause of it...' he came back huskily.

Eva gave an exasperated sigh. 'Do you *ever* give up?'

'Where you're concerned? No.'

Now it was Eva's turn to look wary as she heard the finality in his tone. A warning, perhaps, that Markos's lazy good humour was merely a front, an illusion. As if she needed any warning!

'Why are you even continuing to bother pursuing me when there are dozens of women in New York who would be only too flattered to receive the attentions of Markos Lyonedes?'

He smiled ruefully. 'Because it doesn't work that way.'

She frowned. 'What doesn't?'

He shrugged those broad shoulders. 'I can't speak for other men, of course, but as far as I'm concerned, desire is exclusive to one woman at a time.'

Eva moistened lips that had become suddenly dry. 'That isn't what I've heard...'

Markos scowled. 'Just who the hell have you been listening to, Eva?' he prompted impatiently.

Her gaze avoided meeting that piercing green one. 'It's public knowledge—'

'It's malicious gossip—accompanied by unreliable articles and photographs in newspapers,' he corrected harshly. 'None of which can or should be believed.'

That might be true, but Donna's experience with this man was indisputable—set in stone. Wasn't it?

But no doubt Jack's version of the breakdown of their four-year marriage would differ greatly from Eva's own. There were always two sides to an unsuccessful relationship...

No!

Eva couldn't afford to have any doubts about Markos Lyonedes's callous reputation with women. The physical desire she felt for him already made her feel more vulnerable than she was comfortable with. She had a plan for the rest of her life, and it was a sensible plan— one which did not include an affair for a few weeks with Markos Lyonedes!

'Whatever,' she dismissed uninterestedly. 'I really do have to leave now.'

'But you'll be back on Thursday at six o'clock?'

Eva sighed at his dogged persistence. 'I said I would, yes.'

Markos nodded his satisfaction. Eva might not know

it yet—might not want to know it—but that single kiss they had shared had told him that she wanted him too.

And Markos had every intention of pursuing her until he had her exactly where he wanted her. In his bed.

CHAPTER FIVE

'I totally agree.' Markos grimaced as he saw the look of horror on Eva's face on Thursday evening as the two of them entered the sitting room of what was now his penthouse apartment on the top floor of Lyonedes Tower. He had received a call from Security a few minutes ago, informing him of her arrival downstairs. Most if not all of the Lyonedes employees had gone home now—including Markos's secretary.

'I think bland must have been the middle name of the previous interior designer.'

'I was thinking it's just plain ugly...'

Eva couldn't think what on earth had possessed the previous designer to choose cream and beige as the colour scheme in this beautifully appointed room. The furniture, though obviously expensive, was unattractively square and minimalist, and the only saving grace to this room was the impressive one hundred and eighty degree view of New York, visible from the huge picture windows that covered two of the walls.

Not only was the colour scheme insipid in the extreme, it didn't suit the man who now lived here. Markos's swarthy complexion, dark hair and piercing green eyes required that he be surrounded by the warm colours of the Mediterranean: terracotta, with touches of green and blue, maybe the palest hint of yellow...

Eva brought her thoughts up short as she realised her interior designer instincts had taken over from her common sense. It was two days since she had last seen Markos—two days and two restless nights—during which time Eva had become even more determined that she did not want to spend any more time in this man's company than she absolutely had to. To do so would be opening herself up to all sorts of disappointment. As such, knowing how this room should look was one thing. Being the one to effect those changes was something else entirely.

Of course it didn't help Eva to remain detached and professional to see that Markos was dressed as casually as she was this evening. The darkness of his hair was still damp from the shower, and he had obviously changed out of the formal suit he had worn to work today. He was now wearing a black shirt, the collar unbuttoned at his throat and the sleeves turned back to just below his elbows, with a pair of faded blue denims clearly outlining the leanness of his waist and his perfectly taut bottom and long legs.

She straightened briskly. 'Are the rest of the rooms as awful?'

'Worse.' He grimaced.

Eva found that hard to believe. 'How many rooms are there?'

'Four *en-suite* bedrooms, kitchen, breakfast room, formal dining room, a gym—'

'Okay—a lot.' She grimaced, rummaging through her capacious shoulder bag for her sketchbook and pencil as she continued to look about the room with narrowed, assessing eyes. 'It looks more like an impersonal hotel suite than a private apartment.'

'That's probably because that's what it was designed to be.' Markos shrugged. 'Drakon has his own place in Manhattan. This apartment was used only to entertain business associates in less formal surroundings than the offices downstairs.'

'Do I want to know in what *way* they were entertained…?' Eva eyed him derisively.

'Just drinks and the occasional dinner,' he assured her dryly.

'I'll believe you—thousands wouldn't!'

Markos eyed her ruefully. 'Your opinion of the Lyonedes family isn't very high, is it?'

Eva felt the warmth of colour enter her cheeks. 'I don't know any of you well enough to make a sound judgement.'

'Yet.'

'Ever,' she stated with finality.

'I'll go and make us some coffee while you look round,' Markos suggested lightly.

'Okay.' Eva was relieved to be able to turn her attention to her surroundings as she began to sketch in her pad.

Markos stood for several moments and admired the way Eva's denims clung so lovingly to her curvaceous hips and thighs. The firm swell of her breasts was clearly visible beneath a fitted green blouse, her long dark hair brushed back and secured in a ponytail that made her look younger than her years.

Markos smiled wryly as he realised she had become so absorbed in her work she seemed to have forgotten he was even there. 'Cream and sugar?'

'Fine.' The tip of her tongue was caught between her teeth as she frowned in concentration.

Markos felt his shaft stir at the thought of all the more sensuous uses the moistness of that tongue could be put to. 'Or alternatively I could lie naked on the bed and wait for you to join me?' he said huskily.

'Fine.' Her eyes had a faraway look as she continued to sketch in her pad.

'Or maybe swing naked from the chandelier?' he added with amusement.

'What did you say?' She looked up sharply, her cheeks blushing a fiery red.

'Never mind.' He was still chuckling softly to himself as he walked down the hallway to the kitchen.

Eva felt the warmth of the colour in her cheeks as the rest of Markos's conversation now penetrated the concentration that always enveloped her at the start of a new project.

Except she wasn't going to start a new project.

Was she…?

That certainly hadn't been what she had intended when she'd arrived promptly for this evening's appointment—but one look at the blandness of what should have been a magnificent penthouse apartment and she had instantly been assailed with visions of how wonderful it could and should look.

Still, that didn't mean *she* had to be the one who instigated those improvements…

'Mmm—you were right the other night. Your percolator *does* make a delicious cup of coffee.' Eva gave a satisfied sigh half an hour later, having taken her first sip of the strong brew.

The two of them were now sitting on stools across

from each other at the breakfast bar in the sterile black and white kitchen.

'Now you know where to come the next time you want a decent cup of coffee in the middle of the night.' Seductive green eyes looked across at her in challenge.

Eva straightened, her expression rueful. 'Seems a little extreme when there's a coffee shop directly across the street from my own apartment building.'

'I doubt it has the same fringe benefits,' he drawled.

'Oh, I don't know—the young guy who serves behind the counter at weekends is pretty hot.'

It was Eva's turn to laugh as Markos growled low in his throat, but that laughter faded as she became aware that it was the first time for a very long time that she had felt so relaxed in a man's company she was actually allowing herself to flirt with him. And Markos was the very last man she should be feeling relaxed or flirtatious with!

She straightened on the barstool. 'He's about nineteen years old, and probably not into older women who could do with losing a few pounds,' she said dryly.

'Are you serious?' Markos gave her a disbelieving look.

She gave a perplexed frown. 'Sorry?'

He gave a shake of his head. 'Eva, that nineteen-year-old in the coffee shop probably has his tongue hanging out the whole time he's serving you your coffee!'

She scowled. 'Don't be ridiculous!'

He gave a pained wince. 'Eva, exactly *what* do you see when you look in the mirror?'

'I don't understand...'

Her puzzlement was so totally without guile or artifice that Markos was left in no doubts as to it being genuine. His expression softened. 'Maybe if I were to tell you what I see when I look at you...?'

Eva eyed him warily. 'This conversation isn't going to get insulting, is it?'

'Hardly!' Markos grimaced as he recognised that's exactly what *he* currently was: hard and hot and throbbing, as he always seemed to be when he was in Eva's company. And when not in her company too, if the last two days were any indication. 'Can it be that you really don't know—don't see—how stunningly, incredibly gorgeous you are?'

She shifted uncomfortably. 'Could we get back to discussing a colour scheme for your sitting room—?'

'Let's see.' Markos chose to ignore her change of subject as he looked across at her consideringly. 'Your hair is the colour of midnight—black with a blue sheen—and your eyes—oh, God. I could talk about your eyes all night! They are the colour of the purest gold. Hot—'

'Markos—'

'Molten gold I could happily drown in,' he continued remorselessly. 'And your skin is as pale and unflawed as alabaster. And your mouth!' His voice darkened smokily. 'Would you like me to tell you the things I have imagined those softly sensuous and pouting lips doing to me these past two days?'

The blood in Eva's veins was now pounding as 'hot and molten' as the way Markos had seconds ago described her pale brown eyes, and she shifted uncomfortably as she felt an echoing heat between her thighs, dampening her panties.

Her denims chafed against the arousal nestled there.

An arousal that, until meeting Markos Lyonedes, she hadn't believed herself capable of feeling. An arousal she didn't want to feel. Not for Markos. Not for any man!

Jack had been only too eloquent in his criticisms of her on the day they'd parted for the last time. He had scathingly told her how it was *her* fault he had turned to other women, that she had let herself go since learning they wouldn't have a baby together, that she had always lacked the social graces necessary in his wife, that her hair needed professional styling rather than being left to grow naturally, and that her fuller figure wasn't only unfashionable but a total turn-off sexually.

Oh, Eva hadn't been so without self-esteem by that time that she hadn't known some of his remarks had been made out of pique, deliberately designed to hurt her because she had finally had enough of Jack and his affairs, but that didn't mean his criticisms hadn't hurt, or remained as a vulnerability buried deep inside her.

Which was perhaps the reason why she had decided she didn't need another man permanently in her life.

There was no perhaps about it: her unhappy marriage to Jack and the hurtful things he had said to her that last day were *precisely* the reasons Eva had made the drastic decision not to remarry and to have the baby she craved on her own, through IVF.

And yet she couldn't seem to find the words to stop Markos as he continued gruffly, 'I've imagined you licking and kissing my chest and nipples, your lips and tongue hot and moist as they move down my stomach to my—'

'Markos, please…!' Eva groaned in breathless protest, even as she felt her own nipples ache beneath her blouse. Just from listening to Markos describe having her make love to him? Oh, God…!

His eyes were dark now, burning with the same desire that coursed through Eva. 'But I have not yet finished telling you how beautiful you are.' He gave a self-derisive shake of his head. 'First let me say that you do not need to lose even one pound in weight. You are perfection just as you are,' he added firmly, his voice once again clipped and precise, but this time with forceful decisiveness rather than anger.

She gave a rueful shake of her head. 'I—'

'Eva, there are very few men who actually prefer women with no breasts or hips,' he continued determinedly. 'That is a myth which has been perpetrated by dress designers and by women themselves, I believe.' The darkness of his gaze swept over her appreciatively. 'The fullness of your breasts is exactly the right size to fit perfectly into the palms of my hands.'

'That's only because you have large hands.'

'And all of me is in proportion,' Markos assured her as he reached across the table to clasp one of Eva's smaller hands in his. 'Eva, who told you that you are not sexy and beautiful? What ungrateful, stupid man could ever have told you such lies?'

Eva couldn't breathe. Markos's sensually descriptive words had aroused her to the point where she had briefly dropped the safeguards that had got her through the past five years—the last two years of her marriage to Jack, suffering his numerous affairs, and the past three avoiding any relationship that even *looked* as if it might touch her emotionally.

But Markos was a man who had refused from the first to take no for an answer. A man who was now demanding answers to questions that were too painful for Eva to answer.

She pulled her hands free of his before getting abruptly to her feet. 'Has it occurred to you that maybe it was a woman?' she challenged scornfully, deliberately. 'That maybe the reason I'm not interested in a relationship with you is because I'm not into men?'

Markos sat back on the stool. 'No.'

Eva blinked. 'Just...*no*?'

'Just no, Just Eva,' he drawled dryly.

She eyed him scathingly. 'Is that male arrogance talking?'

'Or the knowledge that seconds ago you were as aroused as I am?'

Her gaze slid down from his, across the rapid and shallow rise and fall of his chest, the flatness of his stomach, down to—

Eva's breath caught in her throat as she saw the thick hard length of Markos's arousal clearly outlined against the press of his jeans.

He hadn't been exaggerating when he'd said that everything about him was in proportion.

'You are so beautiful you make my chest ache, and so desirable you obviously make another part of me ache.'

'Please, Markos—did your years of living in England teach you nothing about our reserve?' she cut in to prevent him making what she was sure was going to be another embarrassing—arousing!—statement.

'Oh, yes.' He walked slowly towards her. 'But fortunately I am Greek, and we Greeks are far less reserved in our appreciation of a woman.'

He was standing so close to her now—just a heartbeat away—that Eva could feel the heat of his body, smell that lemon soap and sandalwood aftershave. That heat and the male smell that was uniquely Markos was now curling about her, invading her senses until she could no longer think straight.

If she had been thinking straight then she would never have allowed this situation to get so completely out of hand. So charged with sexual awareness she could almost reach out and touch it…

Markos drew his breath in sharply at the first touch of Eva's hands against his chest. Her palms seemed to burn through the thin material of his shirt to sear the flesh beneath. His first instinct was to reach out and pull her into his arms before lowering his mouth to claim hers.

His first instinct.

His second instinct warned Markos against moving at all as he allowed Eva's hands to tentatively seek out and touch the hard contours of his chest and the muscled width of his shoulders, sensing that the slightest movement on his part would result in her once again erecting those barriers around her emotions and needs. Barriers some other bastard had instilled in her, which Markos now realised had resulted in Eva hiding her vulnerability behind a mask of spiky cynicism.

It quickly became an agony of self-control for him to withstand the caress of her fingers and palms against and over him. His teeth were gritted, his jaw clamped shut, and his hands were clenched tightly at his sides as he resisted the impulse to reach out and take her into his arms. It was an impulse that became even more painful still as her fingertips ran lightly over the front of his denims, against his thickened length.

Eva's caresses grew bolder as she felt the pulsing response beneath her fingertips, and she knew a deep and compelling need to release that aroused hardness from the confines of Markos's jeans and—

She snatched her hand away before moving back abruptly. 'I think this has gone quite far enough!' Her voice came out husky and breathless rather than conveying the firm resolve she had hoped it would.

Markos groaned low in his throat, wanting, needing so much more, but instead he allowed himself to be guided by those instincts that warned against pushing Eva too far too fast. 'Will you come to a party with me on Saturday evening?'

Startled, she raised her lids. 'What…?'

Markos gave a pained smile in acknowledgement of the fact that his obvious arousal made this the last thing Eva had expected him to say. But he knew that the invitation he *wanted* to make—for her to stay on here now, so that the two of them could cook dinner together—would be met with a blunt refusal. As would his plans for what happened after dinner…

'I have been invited to a party on Saturday evening, and I would very much like it if you would agree to be the guest included on my invitation.'

She blinked. 'You're asking me out on a *date*?'

Markos chose his words with care, having realised in the past few minutes that he still needed to go slowly with this particular woman, that to do anything else would only drive her away. 'I am asking you to accompany me to a party on Saturday rather than leaving me to spend the evening alone in a room full of strangers.'

She shook her head. 'You must know your host to have been invited in the first place.'

'He is a business associate. Nothing more.' Markos shrugged dismissively.

Eva smiled wryly. 'There are sure to be dozens of beautiful women there, so I doubt you'll remain alone for long—'

'And I would prefer to take my *own* beautiful woman,' he interrupted firmly.

Her cheeks warmed. 'I am not your—'

'Eva, please.' Markos cut off her protest gruffly. 'For business reasons I have to attend this party, and for personal reasons I would like *you* to accompany me.'

When he put it like that...

Every instinct of self-preservation Eva possessed told her to say no to Markos's invitation. To stand by her earlier decision to recommend he use another interior designer, and then refuse to see him again.

She should say no. She had to say no. She *must* say no.

'In that case I would be pleased to accompany you. Thank you for asking me,' she heard herself say softly.

Markos chuckled huskily when he saw the chagrined expression appear on Eva's face immediately after she had accepted his invitation. 'Sometimes instinct can be stronger than logic, hmm...?' he suggested mischievously.

'And sometimes instinct can be a complete pain in the—!' She broke off with a grimace. 'I'll meet you here, if that's okay?'

'Because you do not wish me to come to your apartment?' Markos guessed easily.

'Not at all.' She frowned her irritation. 'I'll probably have some preliminary sketches and colour charts to bring over for you to look at by then, anyway,' she added briskly.

It was in an effort, no doubt, to put their relationship back on a businesslike footing. A businesslike footing Markos felt sure Eva had previously decided they wouldn't even be having. Her visit here this evening had been in response to Markos's threat of two days ago rather than any real intention of working for him.

'Bring them, by all means. I had intended to arrive at the party at about nine o'clock, so if you were to come here at eight, that should give us time to look at your sketches before we leave.'

'Fine,' Eva agreed tersely—and realised she had just committed herself to the redesigning of his apartment.

She looked so annoyed with herself for doing so, so irritated, that Markos didn't know whether to laugh or kiss her.

'It is no good, Eva, I have to kiss you again!' He groaned as he moved to put his arms lightly about her waist. 'Just once, hmm?' he encouraged throatily, lowering his head slowly towards hers. She seemed too surprised to protest.

Markos was determined not to send Eva hurtling off into the night this time, so he restrained his need to devour her and kissed her slowly, lightly, tasting her lips as she stood stiffly in his arms rather than giving in to the desire to swing her up into his arms and carry her off to his bedroom.

He kept a tight rein on his control until he felt the first quiver of Eva's response and she began to return that kiss, her lips parting hesitantly as her hands moved up to rest lightly against his chest. It was the most erotic and yet at the same time most frustrating kiss of Markos's life, as he allowed Eva to set the pace of their passion rather than take control as he usually did.

He was finally rewarded for his restraint as he felt Eva relax in his arms and she began to kiss him back in earnest.

Markos groaned low in his throat as he felt the press of her breasts against his chest, the softness of her hips nestling against his arousal. Her hands moved up over his shoulders until her fingers became entangled in the thickness of hair at his nape and the kiss turned hungry.

Markos wrenched his mouth from hers in order to seek out the dips and hollows in her bared throat, his breath moving across her skin in a fiery caress as his hands moved restlessly up and down the length of her spine, igniting trembling desire wherever they touched.

Eva's breasts felt full and hot, and between her thighs she was aching in need for the touch of Markos caressing hands— 'No!' She pushed her hands against his chest and held herself away from him, her breathing ragged and deep as she stared up at him in increasing horror. 'This is not what I want, Markos.'

His arms remained like steel bands about her waist. His eyes were dark green pits of hell, his breathing as ragged as her own as he obviously fought for control. 'What is it you want, Eva? Tell me and it shall be yours,' he promised fiercely.

What Eva wanted was to go back to her previous numbness, to the place where her emotions had been as colourless as the décor in this apartment rather than the blazing colours of fire!

She breathed shallowly. 'I want to collect my things and leave.'

'But you will come back on Saturday?'

Eva knew that she shouldn't—that she should consider running instead, as far and as fast as her car and credit card would take her. Which, considering the money currently in her bank account, was a very long way.

But, having finally stood up to Jack three years ago and put an end to the torment of their marriage, and then remained living and working successfully in New York despite the fact that Jack had made it clear he would rather she returned to England—probably so that he could forget he had ever made the mistake of marrying her in the first place—she had no intention of being forced to leave now just because Markos Lyonedes was making life uncomfortable for her.

She straightened determinedly. 'I'll come back on Saturday.'

'That is good.' Markos's smile was still strained as he indicated she should precede him out of the kitchen to collect her things from the sitting room.

What was good about it? Eva wondered slightly dazedly once she was safely back in her car, driving back to her apartment. It couldn't possibly be 'good' that minutes ago she had been so physically aroused by Markos that she wouldn't have cared if he had laid her down on the coldness of the black and white tiled kitchen floor and taken her right then and there…

CHAPTER SIX

'OH, no…! Markos, turn the car around!'

'What—?' Markos turned his head to give Eva a startled glance from where he sat behind the wheel of his car on Saturday evening, driving them both to the party.

She clutched at the arm of his black evening jacket. 'Turn the car around—*now*—and get us out of here!' she repeated fiercely as she released his arm to stare up in horror at the brightly lit house at the end of the short gravel driveway.

There was already a car in front of them, and one had just turned into the driveway behind them too, effectively blocking any move on Markos's part to do as Eva asked and turn the car around.

'What's wrong, Eva?' He reached out with his free hand to clasp one of hers, instantly aware of how cold that hand was, considering the warmth of the summer evening.

What was *wrong*? Eva had just realised that the party Markos was taking her to was at the home of her ex-father-in-law—that was what was wrong!

Why hadn't she realised sooner?

More to the point, why hadn't she asked Markos on

Thursday whose party it was and saved herself—and Markos—all this embarrassment? As it was, Markos's black Ferrari was now effectively trapped between two other cars, making immediate escape impossible.

Maybe she should just get out of the car and walk back to the city?

Oh, yes, very practical—considering she was once again wearing three-inch-heeled sandals, black this time, to match with the black tube of a dress she wore, in which the length of her legs was very visible beneath the short hemline. Not only was it impractical, but if she tried to hitchhike a ride back into the city she was more likely to be taken for a hooker than a hitchhiker; she doubted too many drivers would recognise the black dress for the expensive designer label silk that it was.

So she couldn't walk back to the city, and she couldn't accompany Markos into the party either. She moistened the dryness of her lips before speaking, still staring at the crowded mansion house in front of them. 'I can't go in there, Markos.'

'Dissatisfied customer?' Markos teased.

Eva smiled faintly at his attempt at humour. 'Not exactly.'

'Then why can't we go to the party?' Markos had parked the car now and turned to look at her in the bright lights of the busy driveway, frowning as he saw how pale her cheeks had become.

The evening had been going so well up until this point. Eva had arrived promptly at Markos's apartment at eight o'clock and, remembering how sceptical she was about compliments, he had deliberately kept his comments as to how stunningly beautiful she looked to a minimum. That figure-hugging black dress, her hair once again loose in blue-black waves about the bareness of her creamy shoulders… Instead he had decided to pretend an interest in the designs she had brought with her.

One look at Eva's designs and he'd no longer had to pretend that interest. They were so vibrant with colour—not a hint of pink in sight, thank goodness!—that Markos had had no qualms whatsoever about allowing Eva free rein with all the rooms in his apartment.

Those initial designs proved that she knew exactly what he needed to feel comfortable in his own home. Perhaps, without realising it, she was coming to know him? Markos certainly hoped that was the case. And he'd been hoping to get to know her better later on tonight…

Consequently they had both been relaxed on the drive over here—only for this to happen. Although at the moment Markos still had no idea exactly what 'this' was!

'Eva, talk to me,' he urged gruffly.

She blinked, those golden eyes having darkened to a deep, deep amber. 'I didn't say *you* couldn't go to the party—'

'I'm not going anywhere without you,' Markos assured her firmly.

'There's no reason why we both have to miss the party—' She broke off as the door beside her was suddenly opened.

'May I help you, ma'am?' One of the young car valets, no doubt hired for the evening, stood outside on the gravel.

Eva's look of panic deepened. 'Markos…!'

He leant over to look out at the smiling teenager. 'Just give us a minute or two, okay?'

The youngster's smile faltered slightly. 'Of course, sir. Except I really need to move your car to the back of the house, with so many other guests still arriving…' he added awkwardly.

Markos sighed his frustration with this situation. Eva was his only concern at the moment. 'You *will* wait—'

'It isn't his fault, Markos.' Eva reached out and put a placating hand on his arm. 'It's okay,' she assured him shakily. 'I'm okay now.'

Which wasn't exactly true. But her initial feelings of wild panic seemed to have settled down to less troubled ones, and now that the initial shock was over Eva knew that most of her residual feelings of unease were only because she had arrived at her ex-father-in-law's home with the powerful and handsome Markos Lyonedes.

She had chanced to meet her ex-father-in-law several times socially in the past three years—it was impossible not to do so when they both remained part of New York society. The difference tonight was that this party was actually in Jonathan's home—the home where Eva had once been welcomed as his daughter-in-law—and also that Eva had never been in the company of another man when the two of them had met in the past.

Not that she thought Jonathan would be in the least unwelcoming—he was far too charming for that to happen, and Markos was his guest after all. Eva was the one who felt distinctly uncomfortable about attending a party at her ex-father-in-law's in the company of a man as powerful and charismatic as Markos Lyonedes.

In the company of *any* man who wasn't Jonathan's own son!

'Eva…?'

She turned to give Markos a reassuring smile. 'I'll be fine now, Markos. Really.' She picked up her black clutch bag before turning to get out of the car.

Eva looked far from fine to him. Her face was still pale, and her eyes still that deep amber and wide with apprehension. But other than making a scene—something Markos was pretty sure Eva would not appreciate—he had no choice but to join her outside on the driveway before handing his car keys over to the obviously relieved young man waiting to park his car.

Markos took a firm hold of Eva's elbow as they walked towards the mansion house ablaze with lights, the rooms visible to them obviously already filled to capacity with other guests. 'Is there anything you want to tell me before we go in?' he prompted softly.

There was a faint sparkle of humour in Eva's eyes now as she gave him a sideways glance. 'Such as?'

Markos had absolutely no idea.

Their host for the evening had been a widower for some years, and was a man in his sixties—surely not someone Eva had ever been personally involved with.

'Don't let your imagination run away with you, Markos,' Eva drawled derisively as she gave him another teasing glance.

'Ah, Markos—so pleased you could make it!'

The smoothly charming voice of their host interrupted them.

Markos instantly felt Eva's tension, and he maintained a proprietorial hold on her elbow even as he turned to face the older man. 'Jonathan.' He nodded stiffly. 'Can I—?'

'Evangeline!' The older man appeared momentarily stunned as he instantly recognised Eva, but that surprise was quickly masked as he once again turned on a politely charming smile. 'How lovely to see you again, my dear.'

'Jonathan,' she returned softly, and the two of them kissed each other lightly on the cheek. 'You're keeping well, obviously.'

'Very much so, thank you,' Jonathan said smoothly, his eyes narrowed shrewdly as he assimilated the fact that Eva was here with Markos Lyonedes. 'Evangeline, I feel I should warn you that the party this evening is— We'll talk again shortly, if that's okay?' he added distractedly as yet more guests arrived noisily behind them. 'Please, go through to the drawing room for champagne and canapés.'

Eva turned instinctively towards the blue and cream drawing room—a room which she had designed for Jonathan four years ago, before her marriage to his only son had come to such an acrimonious end—all the time aware of Markos's brooding preoccupation as he walked beside her, his hand still lightly on her elbow.

He was deservedly preoccupied. Despite Eva's advice to the contrary a few minutes ago, she knew that Markos's thoughts must be running riot as he considered all the possible scenarios for her being acquainted with a man like Jonathan Cabot Grey.

Jonathan Cabot Grey *Senior*.

Because Jack, Eva's ex-husband, was Jonathan Cabot Grey Junior...

'Are you going to tell me what's going on?' Markos

prompted softly once he and Eva were standing beside the unlit Adams fireplace a minute or so later, the two of them having been supplied with glasses of champagne by one of the many attentive waiters circulating the crowded and noisy room. 'Why didn't you want to come in? And exactly what is—or was—Jonathan Cabot Grey to you?' he added harshly.

'Jonathan Cabot Grey was my father-in-law.' Eva was still too distracted by Jonathan's unfinished warning even to attempt to prevaricate, wondering what it was Jonathan had wanted to warn her about. He hadn't sounded in the least threatening, so it obviously had nothing to do with the fact that she was here with Markos. So what—?

'Your *father-in-law*?' Markos repeated incredulously, totally stunned by this unexpected revelation.

She nodded abruptly. 'Cabot Grey was my married name.'

'Of course. Evangeline Grey—Jonathan Cabot Grey...' Markos realised with a pained wince, inwardly kicking himself for not having added two and two together before now.

She shrugged bare shoulders. 'I established my business under the name Cabot Grey Interiors, but dropped the Cabot part after my divorce.'

'So you were married to Grey's son?'

'The one and only,' Eva confirmed, aware that several of the other guests had seen and recognised her now. Their gazes were speculative as they also saw the identity of the dark and handsome man standing beside her. Even in a roomful of other men dressed in evening clothes, Markos stood head and shoulders above them all, in both looks and autocratic bearing.

Eva realised she was grateful for his presence; if she was to be forced to meet any of Jonathan and Jack's friends again then she was glad it was in the company of a man as impressively handsome and wealthily powerful as Markos Lyonedes!

She turned to smile at him regretfully. 'I really am sorry about this, Markos.' She placed her hand lightly on his arm. 'I would never have put you in this embarrassing position if I had known it was Jonathan's party you were inviting me to.'

Markos was still coming to terms with the fact that Eva had been married and divorced. Not that he had anything against divorce; he was of the opinion that it was far better to end something that wasn't right than spend a lifetime of unhappiness with the wrong person. No, it was the thought of Eva having been married at all that disturbed Markos. That left him with so many questions unanswered...

When, and for how long, had Eva been married? Why had the marriage ended? Who had ended it? Eva or Jonathan Cabot Grey's son? And if it was the latter, did she still love the man who had once been her husband?

He drew in a ragged breath. 'Eva, what—'

'Hello, angel.'

Markos found himself as irritated at hearing Eva addressed as 'angel' by another man as he had been the previous week when Glen Asher had called her 'baby'. But even without Eva's hand tightening to a painful grip on Markos's arm at the first sound of that man's voice, a single glance at the man standing behind her would have immediately identified him as being Jonathan Cabot Grey's son.

The hair was golden-blond, where Jonathan's was turning silver-grey, but other than that the family resemblance was unmistakable: blue eyes in similar boyishly handsome faces, both men lean and elegant in black tailored evening clothes.

There was no doubt in Markos's mind that this was the man who had once been Eva's husband.

This was what Jonathan had been going to warn her about a few minutes ago, Eva realised numbly, even as the full force of Jack's presence hit her with the force of a blow.

He shouldn't be here. Shouldn't even be in the States. He had moved to France over a year ago, when he'd taken over the Paris offices of Cabot Grey Enterprises.

Yet it was most definitely him standing just behind her. Even if Eva hadn't known his voice as well as she knew her own, there was no one else on earth who called her 'angel'.

What was she supposed to do now? What was the protocol for introducing your ex-husband to the man you were now…now *what*? She couldn't claim to be dating Markos when this was the first evening they had gone out together, but she knew they weren't only business acquaintances. So what *were* they?

Well, she had better make her mind up—and soon—because the three of them couldn't continue standing in this frozen tableau for much longer.

'Angel?' Jack prompted dryly, obviously coming to the same conclusion.

Eva gave a pained wince as once again he used the name he had once affectionately called her by. A long time ago. A lifetime ago. A different lifetime ago…

She drew in a deep breath and finally looked up into

Markos's rigidly set features. He stared past her at the other man with eyes as hard as the emeralds they resembled, his mouth thinned, jaw tight.

His harshly etched features softened slightly as he finally looked down and saw her expression of mute appeal. 'Introduce us, will you?' he prompted huskily even as his arm moved possessively about her waist.

The gentleness of Markos's tone, and that supportive arm about her waist, instantly reassured Eva that whatever his inner feelings were about this strange situation Markos was there for her now—even if the warning gleam in his eyes also told her that he would expect answers to his numerous questions once they were alone.

Eva turned slowly to face Jack, her expression deliberately non-committal as she took in the subtle changes in his appearance since the two of them had faced each other across a divorce court.

He was now in his mid-thirties, and there were touches of grey at Jack's temples that hadn't been there three years ago. His face was thinner too, with lines etched beside his nose and mouth. Other than that he was still as lean and boyishly handsome as he had always been, and looking every inch the wealthy Cabot Grey heir in his tailored black evening suit and snowy white shirt.

'Markos, this is Jonathan Cabot Grey Junior.' She made the introduction stiffly. 'Jack—Markos Lyonedes.'

Eva knew there was just a hint of satisfaction in her clipped tone as she stated Markos's name. Understandably so, she inwardly defended herself, when the last time she and Jack had spoken for any length of time he had taken great pleasure in telling her all of her faults.

Jack's eyes widened in obvious surprise as the other man's identity registered. 'Mr Lyonedes,' he greeted him smoothly as the two men shook hands.

'Cabot Grey.' Markos coolly returned both the handshake and greeting.

'Please call me Jack,' the other man invited lightly, the smile fading from those narrowed blue eyes as he turned to look critically at Eva. 'You're looking well, angel.'

'Eva looks beautiful,' Markos corrected coldly.

Eva's continued tension against his encircling arm left him in no doubt that this was the man who had somehow succeeded in convincing Eva that she was neither beautiful nor sexy. The very same man who had once been her husband.

Markos wondered under what circumstances Jack Cabot Grey could have made those hurtful and demeaning comments to Eva. Obviously they had not been happy ones, or the two would not now be divorced.

'That's what I meant, of course,' Jack Cabot Grey agreed, with the same smooth charm as his father.

'I'm afraid Jack and I are well past the stage of being insincerely polite to each other, Markos,' Eva dismissed with noticeable brittleness. 'Speaking of which—shouldn't you be cosying up to your father's other guests rather than wasting your practised charm on the uncharmable?' She raised mocking brows and looked challengingly at her ex-husband.

The hardening of those deep blue eyes was Jack Cabot Grey's only noticeable reaction to the taunt. 'I believe Mr Lyonedes *is* one of my father's guests...?'

But Markos was no more inclined to be charmed by this man than Eva was. Basically because he had never particularly liked men with the smooth and, as Eva had already stated, *practised* charm of a politician, but mainly because Markos resented the fact that this man had once been married to Eva. Lived with her. Known her longer and more intimately than any other man ever had.

Or possibly would again.

The tension between Eva and her ex-husband went a long way towards explaining her cynicism about men and relationships. Especially if their marriage had ended as badly as their attitude towards each other would seem to imply.

Markos straightened determinedly. 'A politeness only,' he clipped. 'For obvious reasons Eva and I will not be staying long.' He looked challengingly at the other man.

'Jack, darling...'

Jonathan Cabot Grey Junior avoided meeting Markos's challenge as he turned to smile warmly at the tiny blonde-haired woman who slipped her hand possessively into the crook of his arm as she moved to his side. 'Come and say hello to Markos Lyonedes and Eva, Yvette. Markos, Eva—this is my wife, Yvette.'

Those blue eyes glittered with malice as he deliberately looked at Eva as he made the introduction.

If Markos had thought Eva pale before then she now turned an ashen grey, obviously shocked as she looked at the woman who was Jack Cabot Grey's second wife. Yvette was a little over five feet tall, with glowingly lovely features and shoulder-length blonde hair. The rounded swell at her waistline showed that she was also very pregnant.

CHAPTER SEVEN

'IF you will all excuse me...' Eva turned and hurried blindly from the crowded drawing room as the felt the nausea rising at the back of her throat, only just managing to make it into the ladies' powder room down the hallway and lock herself into one of the two marble-tiled cubicles before she was violently ill.

This couldn't be happening!

On top of every other humiliation Eva had suffered at Jack's hands, his second wife was obviously at least six months pregnant, with a baby that Eva, at least, knew couldn't possibly be his!

Unless—

No, it simply wasn't possible that it was Jack's baby. Jack was totally incapable of fathering a child of his own. And yet Yvette Cabot Grey was undeniably pregnant...

How? By another man? Or by the IVF that Eva was contemplating for herself? If that were the case, the baby Yvette carried wouldn't be Jack's...

That was perhaps the thing that hurt Eva the most. After tests had shown that Jack could never have a child of his own Eva had begged and pleaded with him to adopt, or for him to allow Eva the possibility of becoming pregnant by an anonymous donor. Tearful pleas Jack had always denied, with the disclaimer that he could never love a child that wasn't truly his.

'Eva?

'Markos…' She straightened abruptly as she recognised his voice on the other side of the cubicle door… *inside* the ladies' powder room!

'Are you all right?'

Was she all right? Of course she wasn't all right! Not only had her ex-husband remarried, but his second wife was pregnant with the baby Eva had so longed for herself!

No, she certainly couldn't claim she was 'all right'. But what seemed more pressing right now was that Markos shouldn't be in the ladies' powder room in Jonathan Cabot Grey Senior's house…!

Markos looked at Eva searchingly when she unlocked and opened the door, her gaze quizzical as she stepped out into the carpeted area where ladies usually freshened up. It was now empty of all but the two of them. Deliberately so, Markos having turned several of those ladies away before he stepped into the room and locked the door behind him to prevent anyone else from entering.

'You really shouldn't be in here.' Eva gave a derisive shake of her head as she moved past him to one of the porcelain sinks to wash her hands and face before filling and drinking a glass of water. Her face was still that sickly grey colour.

He raised dark brows. 'You are obviously unwell.'

'That's still no reason—'

'The door is locked, and I will go where I want

whenever I deem it necessary,' Markos declared harshly.

Eva gave a pained wince. He now appeared every inch the arrogantly forceful Markos Lyonedes, joint owner of Lyonedes Enterprises. 'And you deemed it necessary tonight to lock the two of us in a ladies' powder room in my ex-father-in-law's home?'

His jaw tightened. 'Yes.'

That was what Eva had thought he would say. And he was right, of course; she could imagine nothing worse than that anyone else should witness her humiliating reaction to being introduced to Jack's very pregnant second wife. It was enough that Markos must now be wondering why she had reacted so strongly...

She took another sip of water and deliberately avoided meeting Markos's gaze in the mirror above the sink. 'I'm sorry about this. I suddenly felt ill—I must have eaten something earlier that disagreed with me.'

'Or met someone...?' he suggested dryly.

Eva gave a humourless smile. 'Or met someone,' she acknowledged self-derisively.

Even in her distress Eva couldn't help noticing how out of place Markos looked in this ultra-feminine room, with its rose and green floral wallpaper. Even the soaps next to the sinks were the same deep rose colour, and several bottles of expensive perfume and pale pink towelling squares were arranged neatly on the onyx marble top. There were also two comfortable chairs covered in rose-coloured velvet.

'Could we possibly leave now, do you think?'

He nodded tersely. 'I have already asked for the car to be brought round.'

Eva's tensed shoulders slumped with relief. 'Have I mentioned before how wonderful you are?'

'I do not believe so,' Markos answered dryly. 'But I will be happy for you to tell me so once we are well away from here.' His face darkened grimly.

Eva couldn't even begin to imagine how awkward this situation was for Markos. How awful to have brought her here, expecting to spend a pleasant evening at the home of a business colleague, only to learn that business colleague was in fact Eva's ex-father-in-law—and, even worse, that her ex-husband was also here with his second and very pregnant wife…

'Markos, I really am sorry.'

'As I said, we will talk about this once we are well away from here.' He continued to frown grimly as he took a firm grip of her elbow to hold her firmly at his side as he unlocked the door. 'We will leave now.'

She blinked. 'Without saying goodbye?'

Markos nodded abruptly. 'Without speaking to anyone.'

Eva sensed the anger burning beneath the surface of Markos's outwardly calm demeanour as they stepped out into the huge hallway, but she didn't know him well enough yet to know who that anger was directed at: this uncomfortable situation or her.

'Markos—'

'Ah, there you are, angel. Feeling better…?'

Eva's heart skipped a beat at the sound of Jack's voice. Markos's fingers squeezed her elbow reassuringly before the two of them turned to face the other man in the otherwise deserted vestibule of the entrance hall. Eva breathed an inward sigh of relief as she saw

If offer card is missing write to: The Reader Service, P.O. Box 1867, Buffalo, NY 14240-1867 or visit us at www.ReaderService.com.

NO POSTAGE
NECESSARY
IF MAILED
IN THE
UNITED STATES

BUSINESS REPLY MAIL
FIRST-CLASS MAIL   PERMIT NO. 717   BUFFALO, NY

POSTAGE WILL BE PAID BY ADDRESSEE

THE READER SERVICE
PO BOX 1867
BUFFALO NY 14240-9952

Play the Lucky 7 Hearts Game

and get...
2 FREE BOOKS and
2 FREE MYSTERY GIFTS...
YOURS TO KEEP!

yes! I have scratched off the gold card.
Please send me my **2 FREE BOOKS** and
2 FREE MYSTERY GIFTS (gifts are worth about $10).
I understand that I am under no obligation to purchase
any books as explained on the back of this card.

Scratch Here!
Then look below to see what your
cards get you....2 Free Books
& 2 Free Mystery Gifts!

❑ I prefer the regular-print edition
106/306 HDL FS97

❑ I prefer the larger-print edition
176/376 HDL FS97

FIRST NAME   LAST NAME

ADDRESS

APT.#   CITY

Visit us online at
www.ReaderService.com

STATE/PROV.   ZIP/POSTAL CODE

Twenty-one gets you
2 FREE BOOKS and
2 FREE MYSTERY GIFTS!

Twenty gets you
2 FREE BOOKS!

Nineteen gets you
1 FREE BOOK!

TRY AGAIN!

© 2011 HARLEQUIN ENTERPRISES LIMITED. Printed in the U.S.A.

▼ DETACH AND MAIL CARD TODAY! ▼

HP-LH2-08/12

Jack was alone; she wasn't sure she could bear to see the pregnant Yvette again this evening.

'Markos and I are leaving now,' she said coolly.

Jack raised blond brows. 'You only just got here.'

'And now we are leaving,' Markos bit out coldly. 'Please inform your father than I will telephone and speak with him some time next week.'

The other man's cheeks became slightly flushed. He obviously resented Markos's authoritative tone. 'It would be more polite if you were to tell him that your-self.'

'As I am sure you are only too well aware, the cur-rent situation is beyond politeness.' Markos looked at the other man with coldly glittering eyes.

'Markos—'

'Stay out of this, angel!'

Markos released Eva's arm and strode quickly across the hallway until he stood only inches away from the other man. He was slightly taller than Jack Cabot Grey. He was not touching him, but was still intimidating nonetheless.

'Her name is Eva. And you will not speak to her in that way. Ever again! Do I make myself clear?' he grated softly.

The other man's jaw tightened. 'You can't just come into my father's home and threaten me—'

'I believe I just did,' Markos purred softly. Dangerously.

'I call her angel because her name is Ev-*angel*-ine.' Jack Cabot Grey met his gaze challengingly for several seconds before those deep blue eyes slid away and he instead looked at Eva. 'It would seem that your mar-riage to me gave you a taste for powerful men, angel,' he drawled insultingly.

Markos drew in his breath sharply. 'You—'

'I only see one man who fits *that* description, Jack,' Eva cut in scathingly. 'And it isn't you!'

'Why, you little—' Jack Cabot Grey broke off warily as Markos placed a hand against his chest.

'I believe I have warned you never, ever to insult Eva in my presence again,' he reminded him in an icily soft voice.

'What on earth is going on here?'

Eva turned a stricken face to see her ex-father-in-law, Jonathan Cabot Grey, stride forcefully into the vestibule.

Shrewd blue eyes narrowed on his son and Markos Lyonedes as they faced each other challengingly. 'Is there a problem...?'

Markos gave Jack Cabot Grey one last contemptuous glance before slowly stepping away from him to stroll back to Eva's side. He faced his host. 'Eva and I were just leaving.'

'So soon?'

Markos might have been more impressed with the older man's attempt at regret if he hadn't seen the look of relief in Jonathan's eyes before it was quickly masked by polite query. It was a politeness Markos was too displeased to indulge at this moment.

'I am of the opinion that it would have been better if we had left some time ago,' he said dismissively, giving Jonathan a disapproving look as he took a hold of Eva's arm, his mouth tightening with displeasure when he realised she was trembling again as she leant into his side.

What could have happened between Eva and Jack Cabot Grey in the past to have caused this severe reaction in her? For her to be physically ill just from seeing him again?

Except…

Unexpected as it might have been, it *hadn't* been seeing Jack Cabot Grey which had made Eva ill. That had only happened when the other man's second wife had joined them.

Was it because Eva still had feelings for the man, and the existence of that second wife now made reconciliation impossible?

Her scathing attitude towards her ex-husband whenever she spoke to him would seem to imply otherwise. And yet… There was no denying that *something* had made Eva ill just a short time ago. The same something that was still causing her to tremble.

Markos had no idea what Eva was reacting to any longer, and that irritated him as much as everything else about this evening displeased him; he had believed earlier that they were coming to know each other, to like each other—and now this!

'We will speak again later in the week, Jonathan,' he assured the older man stiffly before turning to leave.

'I'll be in touch, angel.'

Eva stiffened as Jack called after her softly, not fooled for a moment by the pleasantness of his tone, and pretty sure she knew the reason Jack intended contacting her again…

Almost as soon as Eva and Jack had married, and had moved to New York to live, Jonathan had started talking of the possible arrival of his grandson—Jonathan Cabot Grey the Third. It was something which Eva and Jack had eventually realised was never going to happen, but Jack had never, at least to Eva's knowledge, confided in his father. The fact that Yvette Cabot Grey was now pregnant, supposedly with Jack's child, was either a medical miracle or something that Jack did not wish Eva to discuss with his father.

Eva didn't know whether to be insulted, because Jack thought she would tell his father that the child Yvette carried couldn't possibly be his, or angry, because Jack thought she would feel vindictive enough towards him that she would deliberately hurt the man who had once been her father-in-law.

The latter emotion won out as she turned to look coldly at Jack. 'We have nothing to talk about,' she assured him scathingly.

He quirked blond disbelieving brows. 'No?'

'Absolutely not,' she snapped, before turning to her ex-father-in-law. 'Goodbye, Jonathan. It was nice seeing you again.' Her voice warmed slightly as she spoke to the man she had always rather liked.

Jonathan must have been surprised when Jack had returned from working in London for two years with Eva as his wife—a young Englishwoman who wasn't in the least wealthy or of the same social strata as the Cabot Greys. But never by word or deed had Jonathan ever shown her anything but the respect and liking due to her as his son's wife. The future mother of his grandchildren...

'Take care,' she added huskily, not sparing Jack so much as a second glance as she and Markos finally left together.

'Not here and not now,' Markos advised gruffly as Eva tried to speak once they were outside.

She shot him a fleeting glance. 'I was only going to say thank-you.'

Markos's tension eased slightly and he relaxed his grip on Eva's arm. The last few minutes had been far from pleasant. For any of them.

'If you insist, you may offer me suitable thanks once we are alone together in my apartment,' he assured her gruffly.

She looked uncertain. 'Your apartment...?'

He shrugged broad shoulders. 'We have to return to Lyonedes Tower in order for you to collect your car. Once there, we might as well go up to my apartment and talk in comfort.'

An argument to which she had no rebuttal, Eva acknowledged ruefully. Her car *was* at Lyonedes Tower, and she did owe Markos a suitable thank-you—although she had a feeling her idea of suitable and Markos's might differ greatly in content! He had been so supportive of her this evening and she owed him an explanation as to the reason he had needed to be so.

'Coffee, wine or brandy?' Markos offered dryly once they were once again in the anaemic sitting room of the penthouse apartment at Lyonedes Tower.

'Oh, I think this situation calls for brandy all round, don't you?' She sighed wearily as she sank down in one of the boxy cream armchairs.

'I am unsure as yet exactly what this situation is.' He shrugged out of his jacket and draped it over a chair, before moving to the bar situated at the other end of the room and pouring brandy into two glasses.

Eva grimaced as she took the glass Markos held out to her before moving to stand a short distance away from her. 'It isn't every day that you meet your ex-husband by accident!' She sipped the brandy, instantly feeling the effects of the fiery alcohol as it slid easily down the back of her throat. 'The last I heard of Jack he was living and working in France.'

'Which is obviously where he met and married Yvette.'

'Obviously,' Eva echoed non-committally as she stared down at the beige carpet.

'Are you still in love with him?'

She gave Markos a startled look and the glass shook precariously in her hand. 'What?'

His smile lacked humour. 'In the circumstances it is a relevant question, I would have thought.'

Eva drank down the rest of her brandy before answering him, in the hopes that its warmth would melt the block of ice that seemed to have formed in her chest. 'What circumstances?'

Markos kept his expression deliberately bland. 'You did not appear to become ill until after the appearance of Grey's second wife. Do not cry, Eva.' All attempts to remain detached fled as he saw the tears shimmering in Eva's huge gold-coloured eyes, and Markos quickly placed his brandy down on the glass-topped coffee table before moving onto his haunches beside the chair where she sat, to take her icy cold hand in his. 'Talk to me, Eva. Tell me why you are crying.'

'I'm not,' she denied, even as those tears began to fall down the paleness of her cheeks. 'I just… You're right. Seeing Yvette…it was a shock—' She broke off and began to cry in earnest.

It was as if a dam had burst inside Eva—the dam that had held back all the grief and pain she had buried deep inside her when her hopes and dreams of having a family of her own, a baby of her own, had been dashed five years ago, when the specialist had told them that Jack could never father a child.

A child Jack now appeared to be having with his second wife.

It didn't matter by what means Yvette Cabot Grey had become pregnant, only that she was. With the baby Jack had denied Eva five years ago.

Markos was completely at a loss as to what he should do or say as Eva buried her face in her hands and sobbed as if her heart were breaking. Which perhaps it was.

Over Jack Cabot Grey?

Having no experience upon which to draw, it wasn't for Markos to criticise whom others might choose—or not choose—to love. Except that Jack Cabot Grey was everything Markos disliked in a man: shallow, selfish and, where Eva was concerned, in Markos's opinion cruelly vindictive. None of which changed the fact that Eva could not seem to stop crying as if her heart were breaking.

Markos reached out and gathered Eva up into his arms, lifting her and cradling her tenderly against his chest before sitting down in the chair himself. Her tears quickly dampened the front of his shirt. Markos ran his fingers soothingly against her temple, considering the irony of holding the woman he desired in his arms as she cried over another man.

If his cousin Drakon could only see him now.

'It was the baby,' Eva finally choked out painfully. 'I—we—we tried for so long to have a baby of our own, and—we finally had tests. The specialist told us it wasn't possible,' she sobbed.

Oh, dear God! And that cold-hearted bastard Cabot

Grey had stood there and calmly introduced his pregnant second wife to Eva, all the time knowing that
Eva wasn't able to have a baby herself. The absolute
bastard!

Could this also be the reason Eva's self-confidence
was so fragile beneath her veneer of derision? The reason she was so determined not to become involved with
another man? Possibly also the reason she and Jack
Cabot Grey had divorced?

Markos could certainly believe the latter. Even on
such short acquaintance Markos knew that Jack Cabot
Grey was the sort of vindictive bastard who would
never have let Eva forget she was unable to give him
the Cabot Grey son and heir.

'It's all right, Eva,' he assured her softly, speaking
into the silky softness of her hair. 'Everything is going
to be all right.'

She gave a choked laugh. 'Of course it isn't.'

No, as far as Eva was concerned perhaps it wasn't…
'You are a beautiful young woman, with all your life
still ahead of you. Not all men are like Jack Cabot
Grey—'

'Thank goodness!' She gave a shiver of revulsion.

Markos looked down at her quizzically. 'You really
do not love him still?'

Eva straightened before attempting to stand up, but
she was prevented from doing so as Markos's arms
tightened about her to keep her firmly sitting on his
knee.

Which was pretty embarrassing, now that Eva thought
about it. In fact the whole of this evening had been embarrassing, she realised, now that she had got over her
shock and calmed down a little.

First of all she had completely flipped out when they'd arrived at Jonathan's house. Then she had almost collapsed with surprise when she had realised Jack was also at the party. Even worse, she had run from the room and been violently ill in the ladies' powder room once she had seen that Jack's second wife was pregnant. An embarrassment that Markos had witnessed when he followed her. And now she had cried all over Markos's white shirt, probably ruining it, no doubt giving him completely the wrong impression as to why she had become so upset in the first place.

Not the best first date she had ever been on.

She doubted Markos had ever had one like it before, either.

She gave a shake of her head. 'I'm not sure that I ever did love Jack,' she answered him honestly. 'Not really.'

'And yet you married him…?'

Eva nodded. 'I was a student when we met at a party given by one of my father's friends. Jack was six years older than me, and he seemed so mature and self-assured in comparison with my other friends— taking me out to the theatre and wining and dining me at expensive restaurants.' She grimaced as she saw Markos's raised brows. 'I've had plenty of time to think about this, and I know now that I allowed myself to be dazzled by Jack's easy charm and self-confidence. I mistook being dazzled for being in love.'

Markos looked down at her quizzically. 'It was a big thing to move to New York with him—away from your family and friends—after you were married.'

'I'm afraid that was probably in an effort to get away from most of my family. My parents aren't the happiest married couple in the world,' she explained at Markos's questioning look. 'They should probably never have married each other, and they certainly shouldn't have had a child together. My childhood was like a battle-field.'

Markos gave a pained frown as this further knowl-edge of Eva's life only added to those reasons why she now felt so cynical towards love and relationships. His own childhood hadn't been without trauma, when his mother and father had died so suddenly when he was only eight, but when he'd gone to live with his aunt and uncle he had been lucky enough to find another set of parents who had loved and cared for him as their own. Whereas Eva didn't seem to have had even one set of parents to love and nurture her.

'You haven't had an easy time of it, have you?' Markos observed.

Eva smiled bravely. 'No worse than a lot of people.' She drew in a deep breath. 'Markos, I seem to be doing this a lot recently where you're concerned—but I really am sorry for blubbing all over you just now.'

'No apology is necessary.'

'What if I were to make it a "suitable" one…?' Eva quirked her brows at him as she pulled his bow tie undone, before starting to unfasten the buttons down the front of his shirt.

Markos regarded her warily. 'I am not sure this is a good idea—'

Eva didn't allow him to finish as she moved to lean into the hardness of his bared chest before pressing her lips against his.

Markos sat completely unmoving, his arms still lightly about Eva's waist as those deliciously sensual lips moved softly against him, as light as butterfly wings. The lightness of her perfume was invading his senses, and he felt the heaviness of her breasts pressing against the hardness of his chest.

She moved back slightly, her palms hot against his chest, her breath warm against his lips as those golden eyes looked directly into his. 'Make love with me, Markos...'

His body reacted instantly to that husky invitation, his pulse racing, heart pounding, and his shaft becoming rock hard and throbbing in seconds. It was impossible for him to deny how much he wanted to accept that invitation.

But he wasn't going to do so.

Eva might have stopped crying, but there was no forgetting how upset she had been earlier. And the reason for that distress wasn't going to go away any time soon—which probably meant she wasn't completely responsible for her actions right now. For Markos to make love with her under these circumstances would surely make him as much of a bastard as her ex-husband. Even if he *did* literally ache to just pick Eva up in his arms and carry her to his bed!

CHAPTER EIGHT

'WHERE are you taking me?' Eva's arms moved up about Markos's neck as he stood up with her still cradled firmly in his embrace.

His eyes were a deep, dark emerald as he glanced down at her. 'Where would you like me to take you?'

'You know...I don't think I really care,' Eva answered, surprising herself with her own honesty as she realised she really *didn't* care where she was going, so long as Markos was going to be there too.

Something had happened to her when that dam of emotion had burst inside her earlier and she had cried in Markos's arms. Somehow—miraculously—she had been released from all past hurts and disappointments, leaving her emotions as light and free as they had been when she was a university student. She felt that same bubbling sense of anticipation inside her now that she'd had then—what might happen in her life next?

What *might* happen—not what had Eva been *planning* to happen? Because she no longer felt that determination to decide her life. She had let go of the past. All of it.

So Jack's wife was going to have a baby? So what? Jack probably wouldn't believe Eva if she were to say the words to him, but it no longer upset her that Yvette was pregnant. She simply wished the two of them every happiness with their future son or daughter, and she had no doubt that Jonathan would be over the moon when his grandchild was born—boy or girl.

One day Eva might even have that for herself—a man and a family of her own to love—but until and if that day came she would feel a contentedness, a calmness, and just wait and see what happened next.

And she really hoped that Markos was going to be part of that more immediate 'next'. She had already known he was as charming and self-assured as Jack had ever been, and Markos was certainly more powerfully charismatic—he'd had to be to have persuaded her to go out with him at all this evening! But after tonight she also knew Markos was kind and considerate, with a quiet strength, caring for her in a way her ex-husband never had. For a brief moment earlier tonight she had really thought Markos was going to pick Jack up by his shirtfront and shake him like a rag doll!

But Markos's strength of character was inborn, not acquired or a veneer—and Eva had never physically wanted a man so badly in her life as she now wanted Markos.

Her arms tightened about his neck as she gazed up at him admiringly. 'You really are pretty wonderful, you know.'

He gave a half-smile. 'Because I am capable of carrying all these extra pounds you believe you possess into my bedroom?'

'It's all perfectly proportioned and in the right places!' Eva gave him a playful punch on the arm, realising as she did so that she still carried her black silk clutch bag.

He gave a disarming grin. 'I believe I have already assured you that I am well aware of that.'

Yes, he had—which was another plus in his favour. Markos seemed to be accumulating pluses in spite of Eva's previous prejudice against him. Too many more of them and she could be in serious danger of falling—

Whoa!

Wanting, aching to make love with Markos was one thing—a big thing, considering he was the first man Eva had wanted to be intimate with since the disintegration of her marriage. But allowing her emotions to become involved was something else entirely.

Markos was a Lyonedes. From a family that was powerful and rich beyond her imagining. More to the point, Markos was a man known for having short and meaningless relationships—not a man that a woman might pin her future hopes and dreams on. A lesson her cousin Donna had learnt only too well...

Donna!

Damn it, with everything else that had happened this evening Eva had forgotten all about her cousin's unhappy experience with Markos!

Had she really forgotten? Or could she just no longer quite accept her cousin's version of what had and hadn't happened between them?

Donna had described him as being wonderful when they were going out together, but turning into a cold and ruthless stranger when he had decided he no longer wanted the relationship. Oh, Eva believed Markos was more than capable of being cold and ruthless—she had seen him being exactly that with Jack earlier this evening—she could just no longer see Markos behaving that way towards a woman. No doubt that was another no-no his Aunt Karelia had instilled in him!

Besides which, the cruel and callous Markos her cousin had described him as being at the end of their relationship would never have had the patience or the inclination to deal with Eva's tears tonight. He would have run a mile in the other direction.

Which left Eva precisely where?

Trusting her own intuition?

She had done that in her life once before, with dire results.

No, that wasn't quite true of the events of seven years ago. At twenty-two, her marriage to Jack had seemed to her like a good way of escaping the vicious circle of her parents' relationship. But she was twenty-nine now, with a successful career and a life of her own. This attraction she felt towards Markos was based on that maturity and success, not on an imagined youthful idealism.

'What are you thinking about?' Markos had been watching the play of emotions across Eva's expressive face for the past few minutes after switching on the bedroom light, realising that she was so lost in thought she hadn't even noticed they were now in his bedroom and he was standing beside his king-sized bed, still holding her in his arms.

She gave him a startled glance as she took in the intimacy of their surroundings, and then that surprise was replaced by a warm and inviting smile. 'Nothing of any importance,' she assured him huskily.

'Sure?'

'Very sure,' she confirmed determinedly.

It sounded to Markos as if she had made her mind up to something—to *do* something—and was determined not to allow anything to make her change it.

All of which confirmed to Markos that the decision he had made a few minutes ago in regard to making love with Eva tonight was the right one.

'Could you pull back the bedcovers?' He lowered her slightly so that she could turn back the brocade cover and the duvet, before lowering her completely onto the bed. Her arms fell from about his neck as he straightened slightly to look down at her. Her hair was an ebony tumble against the cream silk sheets. 'Roll over,' he encouraged gruffly as he took the black bag gently out of her hand and placed it on the bedside cabinet.

'Roll…?'

Markos allowed himself to chuckle softly at the doubtful expression on Eva's face. 'Do not look so worried, Eva; my only intention is to unzip the back of your gown, not to force some strange sexual practice on you.'

Her cheeks were slightly flushed as she glanced at him over the bareness of her shoulder once she had rolled slightly away from him. 'Maybe force wouldn't be necessary.'

Markos drew in a sharp breath even as he bent down to slowly lower the zip at the back of her black gown. That breath stayed caught in his throat as he took in the creamy perfection of Eva's long, naked spine, and revealing the top of a pair of silky black panties.

Markos clenched his hands into fists in an effort to stop himself from touching the creamy length of Eva's bared flesh now so temptingly revealed to him, and a nerve pulsed in his jaw as she rolled over to face him once again, allowing him to lower the gown down over her breasts and the slenderness of her waist, curvaceous hips and long silky legs, before discarding it completely.

Those black silky panties were now the only item of clothing she wore—a perfect foil for the creamy naked swell of her breasts. Full and pert breasts, tipped with rose-coloured nipples, which were swelling, hardening, under the heated intensity of Markos's gaze.

Eva was beautiful everywhere—so very beautiful—and in a way that made Markos ache just from looking at her, from breathing in the sensuous perfume of her skin.

'Markos?' Eva looked up at him uncertainly.

His nostrils flared as he breathed out deeply, before bending slightly so that he could pull the covers gently over Eva's tempting nakedness.

Her eyes widened. 'What are you doing...?'

Markos sat on the side of the bed, securing those bedcovers beneath her arms as he reached up and smoothed the silky hair back from her temples. 'I would very much like to kiss you goodnight, if that is agreeable to you?'

'Goodnight...?'

Markos gave a gentle smile. 'I believe you have already suffered enough excitement for one evening, don't you?'

Eva would hardly call the time she had spent at Jonathan's house earlier this evening exciting—nor the bursting dam of emotions that had followed it! Nor would she compare either of those things to the thrill of just imagining making love with Markos...

'I don't understand.'

He gave a shake of his head, his eyes dark. 'This

evening was a less than happy one for you, and I believe it would be wrong of me to now take advantage of you. As such—'

'But I'm perfectly okay now,' she protested.

'You are *not* okay, Eva,' he insisted flatly, his fingers still lightly soothing against her brow.

But she *was* okay—more than okay, actually—so much so that she couldn't even begin to describe the euphoria she felt at being free from the past. 'Perhaps you're the one that's changed your mind about wanting to go to bed with me after I made such an idiot of myself earlier this evening?'

'I have not changed my mind in the slightest in regard to wanting to make love with you, Eva,' he assured her. 'But, as I have already stated, I would prefer not to take advantage of the fact you are feeling less than your usual feisty self.'

Eva looked up at him searchingly. The sincerity of the expression in his eyes and face was unmistakable. 'Such gallantry isn't doing a thing for your reputation as a womaniser, you know,' she teased huskily.

His expression hardened. 'The thing to remember about reputations is that they are formed by people other than the person whose reputation is under discussion.'

Yes, they were. And the man Donna had described to Eva wouldn't have shown a moment's hesitation in taking 'advantage' of her.

Which left Eva feeling more confused than ever in regard to the enigma that was Markos Lyonedes.

She gave a baffled shake of her head. 'If you have no intention of making love with me then why did you undress me and put me in your bed?'

His expression softened again. 'I believe, if we are to be exact, that I put you in my bed first and then undressed you. And I did so because you are emotionally exhausted and need to sleep.'

'I could have gone home and slept.'

'And tomorrow is another day...' Markos continued softly as if she hadn't spoken at all.

Eva chuckled softly. 'You're supposed to be Rhett Butler, not Scarlet O'Hara!'

He shrugged those broad shoulders. 'It is the sentiment which is important, no matter who says it.'

Yes, it was, and Markos's thoughtfulness in not making love with her tonight had succeeded in throwing Eva's emotions into even further turmoil. As well as making her ache for his touch!

'Where are you going to sleep?'

He shrugged. 'There are three other bedrooms in the apartment that I can use.'

'And if I would rather you stayed here with me...?'

Markos drew in a ragged breath. 'I would ask what I have done to deserve such torture!'

'You've been a perfect gentleman,' Eva assured him firmly. 'And if I ever chance to bump into your Aunt Karelia, I'll be sure to tell her what a credit you are to her.'

'I am gratified to hear it,' he replied dryly. 'And now I believe it is time for you to kiss me goodnight and then get some sleep,' he added huskily.

Eva was only too eager to kiss Markos goodnight, but at the same time as she was totally unsure that sleep would be possible once she had.

'And I am going to return to the sitting room to finish my glass of brandy before taking a very long, very cold shower!'

The grimness of his smile revealed the depth of self-control he was having to exert *not* to make love with her as his head lowered towards hers.

Eva curled her arms up about his neck as their mouths met. She put every shred of emotion she was feeling at that moment into a long kiss. The fondness she felt for Markos. The desire. The aching yearning. Most of all the joy in at last being free of the past and able to feel all of those things...

For Markos.

Markos wrenched away from Eva's tantalising lips, breathing hard as he gently but firmly pulled her arms slowly down his shoulders and chest. 'Enough,' he breathed raggedly, shaking his head as Eva's fingers lingered on the bareness of his chest. 'Please, Eva, I sincerely hope that I am a gentleman, but I know I am not a saint!' A nerve pulsed in his tightly clenched jaw.

Her lips were swollen from the heat of their kisses, her eyes a dark languid gold as she looked up at him. 'Goodnight, Markos.' Her voice was as sultry and inviting as the unhidden longing in those extraordinary eyes.

Markos rose quickly to his feet, so as not to give in to the temptation to throw back the bedcovers and taste those deliciously naked breasts. 'I think I may be in need of more than a single glass of brandy to help me get to sleep!' He stepped away from the bed—away from Eva.

Eva gave an enigmatic smile. 'You know where I am if you don't succeed.'

Markos ran an agitated hand through the thickness of his hair. 'You are not helping, Eva!'

She laughed huskily. 'I don't believe I was trying to...' Her breasts were thrust forward and up as she stretched languidly before once again settling down beneath the covers, those golden eyes gleaming with mischief as her gaze lingered on the obvious bulge in Markos's trousers.

'Temptress!' he murmured achingly.

'Spoilsport!' she came back challengingly.

Markos gave a rueful shake of his head. 'I will take great pleasure in reminding you of that taunt in the morning.'

'Promise?'

Markos sucked in a sharp breath and stared down at her for several long seconds more before turning to walk determinedly across to the bedroom door. He paused in the doorway to turn and look at Eva once more. 'You might want to barricade this door with any of the bedroom furniture you can move!'

Her eyes shone back at him teasingly. 'I'm not the one walking away...'

No, Markos was. And he had more than enough reason to regret it once he had returned to the sitting room. Not even two large glasses of brandy were enough to dispel the knowledge that an almost naked and apparently willing Eva was just a short distance away down the hallway.

'You look—'

'Awful,' Markos finished dryly as he looked across the kitchen the following morning to where Eva stood framed in the doorway. 'Whereas you look...' *Sexy as hell,* Markos acknowledged achingly as he took in her appearance in his black silk dressing gown, which reached almost down to her ankles, and with her hair an ebony tangle about her shoulders. 'Rested,' he substituted wryly.

'Did you sleep in those clothes?' Eva eyed the crumpled white evening shirt and black trousers he had been wearing last night.

'I didn't sleep at all!' Markos grimaced.

Having realised once he had taken a shower the night before that all of his clothes were still in the bedroom where Eva was—hopefully—sleeping, he'd had to put back on the same clothes he had worn to go out that evening. Only to then return and sit in one of the armchairs and stare sleeplessly out at the night sky as it changed slowly from black to grey and then orange as the sun came up and the new day began.

'Perhaps you should go to bed now...?' Eva suggested throatily.

'Coffee?' He stood up now from where he'd been sitting at the breakfast bar, moving across the room to the place he had made a much-needed pot of coffee a few minutes earlier. 'Cream?'

Eva paused for only a heartbeat to look at the broad expanse of Markos's back, turned towards her, before crossing the tiled floor on bare feet, knowing from his avoidance in answering her and his guarded expression before he turned away that any move towards intimacy this morning was going to have to originate from her.

She slid her arms about his waist from behind and leant her head lightly against his suddenly tensed back. 'That was an invitation for you to come back to bed with *me,* Markos.'

He breathed in deeply but didn't turn. 'Are you sure?'

'Very sure...'

'If I go to bed with you now I should warn you it would not be with the intention of sleeping!'

'I'm sincerely hoping not.'

The spoon he had intended using to stir the cream into her coffee landed on the marble worktop with a clatter as he turned quickly and gathered her up into his arms. His mouth came down forcefully on hers.

Hungry didn't even begin to describe the fierceness of the passion that flared instantly between them as Markos's hands became entangled in her hair as they kissed: lips devouring, tongues duelling, their breathing hot and ragged in the silence of the apartment.

Eva ceased to breathe at all when she felt Markos's hand cup beneath the fullness of her breast, the soft pad of his thumb moving in a light caress across the hardened tip. Pleasure instantly spiralled through her and she arched into that caress, causing her to groan low in her throat as it pooled, moistened that already aching apex between her thighs.

His lips left hers to trail across her cheek, moving down the column of her throat, inciting fire wherever they touched. A low moan escaped her as Markos gently pushed aside the black silk robe to take the throbbing tip of her naked breast into the heat of his mouth.

Eva clung to the hard heat of his shoulders as she stumbled back to lean against the kitchen unit. Her knees threatened to buckle beneath her, pleasure coursing through her hotly now, as Markos cupped her other breast. She looked down at Markos's darkness against the paleness of her skin, his dark lashes fanned across his swarthy cheeks as he drew her nipple hungrily between his parted lips. Feeling, watching, as Markos paid homage to her breasts, was the most erotic thing Eva had ever done.

She slipped the unbuttoned shirt from his shoulders and down his arms and he allowed the garment to slip to the marble floor. His shoulders were so wide—much wider than they looked beneath his shirt and tailored suits, and deeply muscled. Proof that Markos didn't spend all his time behind a desk. The muscles in his back flexed with pleasure as Eva's fingers lightly caressed down the length of his spine.

'You're beautiful, Markos...' she purred.

He chuckled softly, the reverberations from that chuckle travelling from Eva's nipple to the pulsing heat between her thighs before he reluctantly released her. The warmth of his breath felt cool against her dampened breast as he spoke softly. '*These* are beautiful.' He took his time kissing each of her swollen and sensitised nipples in turn before looking up at her, his eyes gleaming a dark, deep emerald. '*You* are beautiful, Eva. All over.'

'You haven't seen all of me yet...'

'But I am going to.' It was a fierce promise of intent.

'Here?' Eva looked about at the sterile practicality of the black and white kitchen.

Markos gave a mischievous smile as he also became aware of their surroundings. 'The temptation to drape you decorously on top of the breakfast bar and make you the feast is appealing, but, no, I think I would prefer to be comfortable in bed the first time we make love together,' Markos said with gruff intent.

'The first time...?' Eva echoed throatily.

His eyes glowed that deep emerald. 'You can have no idea in how many locations and in how many ways I have imagined making love with you during my long and sleepless night!'

Her cheeks warmed. 'Show me,' she invited huskily.

'Oh, I intend to!' Markos assured her decisively, and he slid one arm beneath her knees and the other about her shoulders before lifting her up into his arms and marching out of the room.

Eva draped her arms about his neck, not in the least self-conscious when her breasts and thighs were laid bare as the black silk robe fell open, knowing she had been longing for Markos to make love to her since last night.

Possibly since the moment she had first looked across that hotel reception room and seen him looking right back at her...

CHAPTER NINE

MARKOS slowly lowered Eva's feet to the carpeted floor before untying the silk belt about her waist and sliding the robe off her shoulders to allow it to pool at her feet. His breath caught in his throat as he looked down at her lusciously naked body: slender shoulders, full and sloping breasts, narrow waist, lush hips covered by that single scrap of black silk and lace, legs long and shapely...

His heated gaze returned to her face, eyes narrowing as he saw a return of that uncertainty in her expression. Her shoulders had tensed, as if she was waiting for a blow to fall.

'You are beautiful, Eva,' Markos assured her huskily. 'And anyone who has told you otherwise is nothing but a fool!' he added harshly, having no intention of saying Jack Cabot Grey's name and allowing the other man to intrude into their intimacy, while at the same time well aware that the other man had to be the reason for Eva's insecurities about her body. 'An idiot and a fool,' he repeated firmly. 'And I intend to worship every delicious inch of you!'

Eva glowed, feeling beautiful under Markos's admiring gaze. 'Can I finish undressing you now...?'

Markos seemed to cease breathing for several seconds before nodding abruptly. 'Please...' He stepped back.

Eva had never thought of herself as a *femme fatale*—how could she when she'd only ever made love with one man in her life, and even that had become more of a chore than enjoyment?—but there was something deliciously wicked about slowly unbuckling the belt at Markos's lean waist. The bulge pressed against the zip as she slowly lowered it to reveal black boxers beneath. Eva sank down onto her knees in front of him as he stepped out of his trousers.

'Eva!' Markos reached out to tightly grip her shoulders. 'I am not sure—'

'Oh, my...!' She had now stripped off those black boxers to reveal the heavy weight of his jutting arousal, moistening her lips with the tip of her tongue before her head slowly lowered.

Markos gave a strangled gasp, his knees threatening to buckle as he felt the moist rasp of her tongue run the length of his shaft before slowly taking him fully into her mouth.

It was torture. Agony. Of the most exquisite kind!

An exquisite ecstasy that Markos enjoyed for as long as he could without releasing.

'Next time, Eva!' he groaned between gritted teeth as he reluctantly pulled away from her. 'Right now I need to be inside you, before I go quietly and completely insane!'

He reached down to lift her before placing her against the covers and following her down onto the bed, his thigh draped across hers as he claimed those wickedly sensual lips with his own.

Markos claimed her mouth again and again as he cupped and caressed her breasts. Their passion was raised to fever-pitch, their pleasure even more so, before he pulled his lips from hers and once again claimed her nipples with his mouth, kissing and biting as Eva gasped her own pleasure.

Her skin felt like velvet as his hand caressed the curve of her hips, slipping beneath the silk material of her panties. His fingers sought and found her sensitive spot, and Eva's response was instantaneous as he caressed that throbbing clitoris, before dipping one finger into the moistness of her channel and trailing that moisture over and around that fiercely pounding arousal in an ever-increasing rhythm.

He gave a low groan even as Eva purred deep in her throat, as she began to thrust her hips up and into that rhythm, her breathing becoming rapid and laboured as her pleasure rose.

Had Eva ever known such hot, mindless pleasure before? She didn't think so. She felt truly beautiful in Markos's arms as he had worshipped every inch of her, and her pleasure had spiralled out of control the moment she felt his mouth and tongue on her, her own movements instinctive as she rose up to meet those moist thrusts.

'Oh, God, Markos…!' She cried out her need as his hands moved up to cup her breasts, squeezing her nipples with just the right amount of pressure between pleasure and pain. The volcanic heat of her rapidly approaching climax was coursing through her like molten lava.

Markos looked down at her with hot and heavy eyes. 'I want to taste you as you come…' He slid down the length of her body until he lay between her parted and silken thighs, claiming her with his lips.

'Markos!' Eva cried out as her pleasure intensified to an unbearable degree. Wave after wave of pleasure washed over her, and she closed her eyes as she gasped and trembled, her fingers curled like talons into the sheet beneath her as Markos refused to release her from that plateau until he had extracted and given every last vestige of pleasure.

'Dear Lord…!' Eva collapsed back against the pillows, her smile dreamy as she held out her arms to him. 'Come up here.'

Markos kissed his way slowly up her body. 'Now I can say with full authority that you are truly beautiful all over,' he assured her gruffly.

'I want you inside me, Markos. I *need* you inside me,' Eva invited huskily. 'Please.'

Markos chuckled his satisfaction as he moved over her, his smile fading as Eva's hand moved down between them and he felt her fingers close about him before she guided him in. He groaned as he slowly entered her, inch by pleasurable inch, until he was sheathed to the hilt.

Which was the moment when Markos's already shaky control broke completely, and he captured her mouth with his as he began to thrust into her with long, claiming strokes, her tightness rippling and clenching about him as he drove into her fully again and again.

He wrenched his mouth away from hers and cried out as her hands caressed the length of his back. Her fingers suddenly dug into the flesh of his backside, and the intensifying ripples of her body told Markos that she was about to climax for a second time.

And Markos intended going with her this time.

He thrust harder, longer, allowing his control to slip completely, shooting hotly down the length of his shaft in a long and satisfying release that shook him to his very soul—and his pleasure was intensified by knowing he had taken Eva with him as her cries matched his own.

'Wow.'

Eva gave a satiated chuckle at the understatement. Markos's head lay pillowed against the fullness of her breasts, and both of them were breathing raggedly in the aftermath of their earth-shattering lovemaking.

It had certainly been earth-shattering for Eva, and Markos's exclamation gave her every reason to believe he had been equally affected. 'Was it worth suffering a sleepless night for?' she teased.

'Most definitely,' Markos assured her with feeling, knowing there had been no ghosts from the past standing between them this morning—just the two of them making exquisite, perfect love. It had been a lovemaking of such tenderness of feeling, with an intensity of pleasure Markos had never experienced before...

Eva tensed in his arms. 'Markos—'

'I believe, if I wish us to spend the rest of the day in bed together, that it is time I fed you.' He lightly interrupted the uncertainty of her tone, sitting up and swinging his legs off the side of the bed and standing up.

'The rest of the day...?' she repeated slowly.

Markos chuckled at the contrasting emotions of surprise and anticipation he could see in those expression golden eyes. 'You did not think that I would allow you to leave after making love with you only once?' He bent down to collect his black silk robe from the bedroom floor.

'I haven't been able to think at all for some time...' Eva trailed off as she gazed up unabashedly at the nakedness of Markos's back, ceasing to breathe as he stretched, the muscles in his back flexing and relaxing with the effortless ease of a jungle cat.

'Good.' He nodded with satisfaction as he turned, his gaze once again becoming hot and heavy as he saw the open hunger she knew must be in her expression. 'Food first,' he repeated firmly, and he laid the black silk robe down beside her before striding determinedly—still naked—from the bedroom.

Eva lay on the bed for several minutes longer, luxuriating in a feeling of total physical satisfaction as she stretched, feeling the pleasurable ache of muscles long left unused.

Making love with Markos had been unlike anything Eva had ever felt or known before. More erotic, more pleasurable than anything she had ever experienced with any man.

There was no point in not being honest with herself at this point in her life. The only other man she'd ever had sex with was Jack. And sex with him had been more centred on his pleasure than hers. Whereas Markos—

She mustn't allow herself to blow this time with Markos out of all proportion.

Not unless she wanted to be left as heartsick as her cousin Donna when whatever this was with Markos came to an end...

She was an independent, sophisticated twenty-nine-year-old woman. They were the things that had attracted Markos to her. No matter how wonderful their lovemaking, he certainly wouldn't want that independent, sophisticated twenty-nine-year-old woman making a fool of herself over him!

Accept this for what it is, Eva told herself firmly as she finally got out of bed to go into the bathroom and tidy herself: wonderful sex, teasing banter and a good time had by all. For her to expect anything else from Markos was totally unacceptable.

Having feelings for Markos certainly wasn't an option…

'So as a child you spent most of your summers on the family's private island in the Aegean?'

Markos nodded, having returned to the bedroom long enough to pull on faded denims and a black T-shirt, totally relaxed as he and Eva sat at the breakfast bar eating warmed croissants with honey and drinking coffee. 'Drakon and Gemini are there now—on their honeymoon.'

Eva gave a wistful sigh. 'It sounds idyllic.'

Markos quirked one dark brow. 'I believe you mentioned your own childhood was less so?'

She shrugged narrow shoulders, the movement instantly drawing Markos's gaze to the way the firm swell of her breasts was revealed as the black silk of his robe parted slightly. 'My parents should never have married each other, and they probably wouldn't have done if my mother hadn't been expecting me.' She grimaced. 'Needless to say they didn't make that mistake again, which is why I'm an only child.'

Markos frowned. 'But you have other family…?'

Eva lowered her gaze as she began to crumble a

croissant on her plate. 'An aunt and uncle…a couple of cousins. And we aren't exactly big on family reunions; I haven't been back to England once in the last seven years.'

Unlike the Lyonedes family. There had been over three hundred guests at Drakon and Gemini's wedding the previous month, and almost all of them had been related to the Lyonedes family in some way.

'I can't even begin to imagine what it must be like not to have a huge extended family,' he said.

'It isn't so bad.' Eva gave another shrug. 'Not enough people to have a big family fallout, for one thing!'

'The Lyonedes family can certainly be volatile,' Markos acknowledged dryly.

She smiled. 'Must be all that hot Mediterranean blood!' Her cheeks coloured hotly as she seemed to realise what she had just said. 'I meant—'

'I know what you meant, Eva.' Markos chuckled at she blushed. It was an endearing and unexpected quality in a woman in her late twenties who had been married and divorced, had lived in New York for the last seven years, and ran her own very successful interior design company. 'And I believe you once implied that you thought Drakon cold when you met him?'

Eva was beginning to wish she had never continued this particular conversation! 'You must have realised after last night that my judgement of a man's character isn't all that good—oh, good Lord!' She winced as Markos raised one mocking brow. 'I obviously wasn't referring to *you* when I said that—what I was really trying to say was—' She broke off with an irritated frown as Markos began to chuckle. 'It isn't funny!'

'I couldn't agree more.' He was still smiling as he

stood up slowly to move around the breakfast bar until
he stood beside her. 'Obviously I need to take you back
to bed and refresh your memory as to how *un*-cold my
own character is…'

He held out his hand, very dark and handsome with
his dark hair still slightly ruffled, his jaw unshaven,
and the tight-fitting black T-shirt outlining the muscles
of his chest and flat abdomen.

'So soon…?' Her eyes were wide.

Markos eyed her quizzically. 'You would rather
not…?'

'I didn't say that!' she protested instantly, her nipples having noticeably tightened beneath the black silk
robe, and that moist warmth once again heating between her thighs. 'I just— I'm just surprised that you—
well, that—'

'That I would, or could, want you again so soon?'
Markos finished huskily, his eyes dark with intent.
'Come back to bed, Eva, and let me show you how
much and in what ways I want you!'

Eva felt slightly shy as she placed her hand in
Markos's and stood up to accompany him to the bedroom. A ridiculous feeling after the intimacies the two
of them had shared earlier.

The intimacies they were about to share again…

'You may just succeed in killing me with pleasure,
Eva!' Markos groaned as she collapsed on top of him
a long, long time later.

'Not intentionally, I assure you.' Eva chuckled
weakly as she lay against the dampness of his hair-
roughened chest, having totally lost count of the num-
ber of times and in how many ways Markos had brought

her to climax—before she had gently pushed him back against the pillow and made love to *him*, first kissing his chest and the flatness of his stomach, before moving lower to take him into her mouth. Her fingers had encircled him as she'd licked that responsive length, until Markos had begged her to stop and she'd moved up to straddle his hips, taking him deep inside her, inch by pleasurable inch, before riding him—riding them both—to explosive pleasure.

His arms encircled her as he rolled to one side and took her with him. 'What *are* your intentions towards me?' he prompted gruffly.

Eva's heart gave a leap even as she opened one wary lid to look up at him. 'Entirely dishonourable, I assure you,' she said softly.

Markos felt a sense of disappointment in Eva's answer, even though he held her in his arms and had every intention of doing so for the rest of the day. And tomorrow…? Tomorrow, as he had already stated, was another day…

'Markos?'

He gave a relaxed smile. 'We will sleep now and talk later,' he encouraged huskily, and he rested her tousled head more comfortably against his shoulder before settling back against the pillows.

'Talk about what?' she prompted, that earlier wariness now back in her voice too.

'Whatever needs to be talked about,' Markos dismissed lightly, and he closed his eyes, Eva still held firmly in his arms.

Eva lay awake for a long time after she knew by the soft and even tenor of Markos's breathing that he had fallen into an exhausted sleep—hardly surprising when he'd confessed to having had no sleep the night before, and then embarked on two athletic bouts of exquisite lovemaking.

Amazingly wonderful lovemaking, during which Eva knew she had lost all and every inhibition she had ever had as Markos touched and kissed her in places she had never been touched or kissed before…

She felt…*wonderful.* Deliciously satiated. Every part of worshipped. And for once in her life Eva intended to let tomorrow take care of itself.

She had no idea whether it was day or night when she woke up, although the brightness of the sun shining through the bedroom window would seem to indicate it was probably late on Sunday afternoon.

Amazing.

She had never ever spent the whole day in bed with a man. And this was not just any man, but Markos Lyonedes.

She turned her head sideways on the pillow to look at him, smiling warmly as she saw that Markos was doing exactly the same thing. Those green eyes gleamed appreciatively, and the stubble was darker on his square chin, his hair tousled on his forehead, his muscled shoulders bare above the bedcovers.

'Good afternoon,' she greeted him huskily.

His eyes crinkled at the corners as he returned her smile. 'Did you know that you purr in your sleep?' he asked.

'You're making that up!' Eva refuted indignantly, her cheeks warming as she turned fully to face him.

'No, I'm not,' he assured her indulgently as he

reached out to touch the hair at her temple. 'You sounded like a contented kitten.'

That was probably because she felt like a contented kitten: warm, intensely satisfied and safe.

Safe?

How could she possibly feel safe when she now knew that Markos was capable of breaching every barrier she had ever placed about her bruised emotions?

And yet that was exactly how Eva felt—safe, cared for, even cherished. So unwise when it came to this particular man! Eva knew better than most how ephemeral Markos's relationships had been and always would be, and she had no intention of falling for a man who chose to fill a woman's life before leaving it—and her—totally empty when he chose to walk away. She had already been burned so very badly once in her life. She certainly didn't need—

'You are thinking again,' Markos rebuked gently, as his fingers moved to smooth the frown from Eva's creamy brow. 'Perhaps it is time for more food...?'

'Good idea.' Her smile didn't reach those golden eyes as she turned away to throw back the bedcover. 'If you don't mind, I think I'll go and take a shower while you look for something to eat.'

She picked up the black silk robe and shrugged into it in such a way that Markos couldn't see her nakedness, before standing up to tie the belt tightly around her waist.

'I can't say I exactly like the idea of going home in a black silk evening gown in the middle of the afternoon!' She wrinkled her nose in distaste.

Markos lay relaxed against the pillows as he looked at her from between narrowed lids, one of his knees bent and raised as a shield to the rampant hardness of his arousal. One look at a tousled Eva when he woke up, along with listening to those soft little purring noises she made in her sleep, and that part of him had immediately perked up and taken an interest!

'Who said anything about your going home in the middle of the afternoon...?'

Eva frowned as she looked across at him uncertainly. 'I think I've already been here long enough, don't you?'

Markos gave a shrug. 'I have no other plans for the rest of the day. Do you?'

'Well...no, not exactly.' She shifted uncomfortably, obviously having no idea how the silk material of robe once again outlined the fullness of her breasts. 'I do have to things to do before work in the morning, though.'

'Such as?'

Eva frowned. 'How about I take a shower and we talk about this again afterwards?' she said briskly. 'I'd really like to freshen up now.'

As it was almost twenty-four hours since Markos had last taken a shower, he could perfectly understand Eva's need to freshen up; he could do with a shave and a shower himself.

'You'll find a spare toothbrush in the bathroom cabinet.'

Eva raised dark, mocking brows. 'Really?'

Markos could almost see the cogs of her imagination turning. 'There's also a spare razor in there—but you really shouldn't infer anything from that!' he drawled dryly.

Colour flared in her cheeks. 'Very funny!'

Markos gave another shrug. 'Just in case you were wondering.'

'I wasn't!'

Oh, yes, she most definitely had been. And Markos knew it hadn't been in a good way. 'What have I done since we met to give you the idea I make a habit of bringing women home to spend the weekend with me?' He moved up on one elbow to look at her from between narrowed lids.

Nothing since the two of them had met, Eva accepted. His pursuit of her this past week or so had been completely single-minded. But she couldn't allow herself to forget his reputation of coldness towards a woman once he had decided he no longer wanted them in his life. As with her cousin Donna.

'Nothing at all,' she dismissed lightly. 'Is this the bathroom over here?' She indicated the closed door on the right of the bedroom.

Markos shook his head. 'The dressing room. Where you will find several of my shirts hanging up if you don't want to put your dress back on.'

Eva tensed at the idea of the intimacy of dressing in one of Markos's shirts. 'Er—no. I'll be fine in the dress, thank you.'

Markos continued to look at her for several long seconds before giving an abrupt nod of his head. 'In that case, that's the bathroom over there.' He nodded at the closed door to the left of the room.

Eva avoided meeting that piercing green gaze as she grabbed her dress up from the carpeted floor, where it had been dropped the night before; no doubt she was about to go home in a very crumpled black silk evening dress!

'Thanks.' Her chin was high as she hastily left the bedroom.

Markos remained laying in bed for several minutes longer, listening as Eva turned on the shower. A large part of him—that hard and rampant part of him!—wanted to get out of bed and join her in the shower to make love with her again, but the more cautious part of him warned that Eva needed a few minutes alone, that—incredibly—her embarrassed awkwardness earlier this morning, and again just now, gave every indication that spending the day in bed with him had been completely out of character.

Reading between the lines what Eva *hadn't* said last night, Markos could well imagine that her marriage to Jack Cabot Grey hadn't been what the English called 'a bed of roses'. So much so that Eva had fought shy of becoming intimately involved with anyone since her divorce.

Markos frowned as the music of Mozart interrupted his train of thought. The sound was coming from inside Eva's evening bag, where it lay on the bedside cabinet, and was obviously the ringtone of her mobile phone.

He glanced towards the bathroom door, wondering briefly if he should go and tell Eva that she had a phone call, and then dismissed the idea as he thought of how she had almost run from the bedroom—from *him*. The sound of water still running told him that Eva was still in the shower. If the call was important then whoever it was would either leave a message or ring back.

Markos's thoughts came to an end as the music stopped just as abruptly. As he'd thought—whoever it was would call back.

Mozart began to play a second time.

The caller was either very persistent, or the call was an emergency. After Jack Cabot Grey's parting comment to Eva last night Markos could easily guess who the persistent caller might be, and having Eva talk to her ex-husband now was guaranteed to hasten her departure. But if it *was* an emergency—

Damn it, he'd answer the call and take the flak from Eva later for doing so!

The name of the caller on the lit screen of Eva's mobile phone made his eyes widen in surprise.

CHAPTER TEN

Eva felt more than a little awkward when she entered the kitchen half an hour later. Her hair was still damp from the shower and she wore no make-up, although she had accepted Markos's invitation and borrowed one of his shirts from the dressing room—a cream silk. She felt less conspicuous wearing the shirt over her figure-hugging evening gown like a jacket, the sleeves turned up to just beneath her elbows.

Markos had obviously been busy in her absence. A salad and a selection of cheeses were laid out temptingly on the breakfast bar, and she could see from the dampness of his dark hair and clean-shaven jaw, as he turned to look at her from beneath hooded lids, that he had also taken a shower and freshened up in one of the apartment's many other bathrooms. He was wearing black denims and a fitted white T-shirt which emphasised both his muscled chest and the natural tan of his skin. Markos looked more edible than the food!

This was not what Eva wanted to feel after deciding earlier on today that she was going to be sophisticated and casual about all this, and not try to make it into something it wasn't. As far as Markos was concerned, anyway. Eva would have time to sit and decide how she felt about it once she was safely back in her own apartment.

The guarded look in Markos's expression as he put a basket of freshly baked bread on the breakfast bar before sitting down on one of the stools only served to confirm that Eva needed to act cool as well as sophisticated.

'This all looks delicious!' she complimented him brightly as she sat on the stool opposite him. 'I'll just eat a little something and then I really do have to leave.'

His expression was still guarded. 'I thought we could talk first.'

Eva avoided his piercing green gaze as she concentrated on breaking open a piece of the crispy bread. 'I'm not really one for post-mortems, are you?' she dismissed lightly. 'We had fun together. Let's just leave it at that.'

Markos looked across at her. 'Can we do that?'

She gave him a startled look. 'Sorry...?'

Markos leant his elbows on the breakfast bar and continued to stare across at her. 'You had a telephone call earlier when you were in the shower.'

Her eyes widened, her thoughts racing at Markos's continued aggression. 'And you answered it...?' If Jack had carried out his threat to 'be in touch...'

'No.' His eyes glittered through narrowed lids. 'I decided not to after seeing the identity of the caller on the display.'

Eva moistened suddenly dry lips. 'And...?'

'And it would seem that you forgot to mention we have a mutual acquaintance,' he commented mildly. Too mildly.

Eva gave up all pretence of putting food on her plate and straightened warily. 'We do…?'

'Yes,' Markos rasped.

She gave a puzzled shake of her head. 'I'm afraid you're going to have to be a little more explicit than that if you expect me to know what you're talking about.'

Markos stood up abruptly, too filled with impatient restlessness to sit at the breakfast bar any longer. 'I am curious to know why you have not mentioned that you are acquainted with Donna Cresswell—the woman who you surely know was my PA in London until a few weeks ago?'

'Ah.'

'Yes—*ah*,' Markos bit out evenly, not in the least comforted by the way the colour had leeched from Eva's cheeks.

To say that Markos had been surprised to recognise the name of the Englishwoman making the call to Eva's mobile phone earlier was putting it mildly. It was the same Englishwoman who had once been his PA—a PA he had been forced to dismiss some weeks ago under less than pleasant circumstances.

Eva's obvious dismay now only seemed to confirm his earlier suspicion that perhaps this was the reason behind those two cancelled appointments made by interior designer Evangeline Grey, and behind her dismissive manner towards him the evening Markos had introduced himself to her at Senator Ashcroft's cocktail party. He also strongly suspected there was a distinct possibility Donna Cresswell might have told her friend Eva a different version of those events of six weeks ago.

'The two of you are friends…?' he prompted evenly.

She swallowed before answering. 'Cousins.'

Cousins? Eva and the machinating Donna Cresswell were *cousins*?

Markos's thoughts were now in such disarray he had no idea what to think about this less than welcome revelation. 'I thought you said yours was not a close family.'

She flinched. 'It isn't.'

'With the exception of yourself and your cousin Donna, it would seem?'

Her gaze avoided meeting his. 'We aren't exactly what I would call close, either. We saw a lot of each other when we were children, but not so much any more.'

'But you are still close enough that you exchange regular telephone calls?'

'Occasional telephone calls,' she corrected distractedly.

His nostrils flared. 'And your cousin never mentioned to you the name of her current employer during these "occasional" telephone calls?'

'Well, of course she mentioned you!' Eva eyed him exasperatedly.

'And what, exactly, did she say about me? From your earlier attitude towards me nothing complimentary, I would guess.' His mouth twisted scathingly.

'Considering the way things ended so badly between the two of you—'

'Badly?' he repeated harshly. 'I had to dismiss your cousin for behaviour that was not only unprofessional but also less than acceptable to me personally!'

Eva frowned. 'Admittedly Donna should have had more sense than to fall in love with you, but I would hardly call that—'

'Eva, I have no idea what your cousin has told you

of our past…association, but I somehow doubt, from your comment just now, she can have mentioned that I was less than pleased the evening I returned to my hotel suite and found her naked in my bed!' His eyes darkened angrily at the memory.

Eva's frown was pained. 'If that really happened—'

'Oh, I assure you it did!'

'Then I agree. It wasn't the wisest move on Donna's part.'

Eva grimaced, having had no idea until that moment of the extremes her cousin had gone to in order to try and revive her relationship with Markos. Although it *did* sound like the sort of thing Donna would do…

'But it was hardly grounds for dismissal, when she was obviously only reacting to the fact that she was so unhappy you had ended your personal relationship.'

His brows rose into his hairline. 'We did not *have* a personal relationship.'

Eva stilled at the vehemence of his tone. 'Sorry?'

'Your cousin and I did not have any relationship other than the fact that she was—briefly—my employee,' Markos repeated evenly.

Eva looked at him searchingly. The angry glitter of his eyes and the tension in his jaw were enough to assure her that Markos was telling the truth. The truth as he saw it, at least…

'Markos, you aren't the first man to make the mistake of having an affair with an employee which results in awkwardness once that affair is over—'

'Eva, what did you not understand about my previous statement?' he cut in exasperatedly. 'I have not been, and will never be in the future, personally involved in any way with Donna Cresswell.'

Eva blinked. 'But Donna said—'

'After the things she screamed at me the night I had to dismiss her from my employment, I can all too easily imagine what your cousin said about me, Eva.' Markos began to pace the kitchen restlessly. 'I can only say— once again—that my feelings towards your cousin were never anything other than the polite regard of an employer. And even that ceased the moment she decided to put herself naked in my bed!'

Eva swallowed hard. She'd begun to feel nauseous. 'But…'

'Yes?'

Could Donna have lied…?

The possibility of that having been the case was so strong that Eva felt as if the ground had just dropped out from beneath her feet. Eva had seen Markos arrogant, even haughty on occasion, but never coldly, chillingly angry—as he undoubtedly was now.

So much so that he bore little or no resemblance to the man who had treated her so gently the night before, or made love with her such a short time ago.

But what possible reason could Donna have had for lying to Eva about having a relationship with Markos Lyonedes?

Eva thought back to her childhood, to the family occasions when she and Donna had been together—those weekends they had both spent with their grandparents. Eva hadn't thought of them for years, but now she belatedly recalled how Donna had always had to have a bigger or better toy than her, or have attended a more fun or glamorous birthday party.

Better. Bigger. More glamorous.

And a relationship with the charismatic Markos

Lyonedes would no doubt have sounded so much more than even Eva's marriage to the wealthy American Jonathan Cabot Grey Junior…

'Donna lied,' she stated flatly.

'Oh, yes, she most certainly lied if she claimed the two of us were ever intimately involved,' Markos confirmed softly. 'What I wish to know is how, and to what extent, those lies have affected your own behaviour towards me?'

Eva gave him a startled look. 'I don't understand…'

'Oh, I think you do, Eva,' Markos bit out grimly. 'And I think your family connection to Donna Cresswell more than explains the little game you played with me at the beginning of our acquaintance.'

She moistened her lips with the pink tip of her tongue. 'I was predisposed not to like or trust you, yes—'

'A fact you made more than obvious!' Markos frowned as he recalled the way Eva, as interior designer Evangeline Grey, had made and then cancelled two appointments with him in a week. She had been scathingly dismissive of him, even insulting, on the evening the two of them had met at Senator Ashcroft's cocktail party, and had made that cryptic comment concerning his 'reputation'. Believing the lies her cousin had told her about him would certainly explain that remark!

'The question is, Eva, how do you feel about me now that we have come to know each other better?'

She gave him a startled glance before focusing that wide golden gaze somewhere over his left shoulder. 'How do I feel about you?'

'Yes!' A nerve pulsed in his tightly clenched jaw. 'Now that we have spent time together—talked, made love—what are your feelings towards me?'

Eva gave a pained frown, knowing she couldn't deny that she had initially behaved in exactly the petty way Markos suspected she had. Quite when her feelings towards Markos had changed from scathing dismissal to a grudging liking Eva had no idea, but she had known last night, when he'd behaved so protectively towards her in regard to Jack, that she not only liked him—a lot—but also that she desired him too. It was a desire the two of them had acted on earlier today—several times.

But the chances of Markos believing that, now that he knew of her family connection to Donna—the woman who had not only completely invented a relationship with Markos, but had also lied to Eva about the callous way Markos had brought that non-existent relationship to an end—were exactly nil!

At least they were if Eva didn't want to totally humiliate herself and tell Markos how much, and how deeply, she now liked him—perhaps more than liked him. Which was *definitely* something she needed to think about once she was alone in the privacy of her own apartment.

Eva forced a rueful smile. 'I believe I told you earlier my intentions are entirely dishonourable!'

He gave a humourless smile. 'In exactly the way you have imagined my own were in regard to the women who have shared my bed in the past? Women who would, if asked, confirm that I have never deliberately, knowingly, hurt any of them. No matter how much the gossips or newspapers might have chosen to sensationalise those relationships. Certainly I have never behaved towards a single one of those women in the cruel and heartless way that your cousin appears to have claimed I treated her.'

'I believe you—'

'Do you?' he questioned sceptically. 'Do you *really* believe me, Eva? Or do you still think your suspicions in regard to me to have been justified? Enough, perhaps, for you to have decided to give me a dose of my own medicine?'

Her eyes widened. 'Are you implying that I might have *deliberately* gone to bed with you with the intention of—of—?'

'I have absolutely no idea what today was about.' His eyes glittered intently. 'Why did you go to bed with me, Eva?'

'I don't—' She gave a dazed shake of her head. 'You were kind to me last night—'

'And do you always spend the day in bed with men who are *kind* to you?'

Her face was very pale as she answered him quietly, 'There really haven't been that many.'

'Men in your bed? Or men who have been kind to you?'

Both, as it happened, Eva acknowledged heavily. Just as she acknowledged that this conversation had now deteriorated to such a level there was surely no hope of the two of them continuing a relationship.

'Eva, talk to me, damn it!' Markos hands were clenched into fists at his sides. 'Help me to understand what happened between the two of us earlier today.'

She released a heavy sigh. 'Can't we both just accept that we made a mistake—?'

'Is that truly what you believe?' He stood still as a statue and looked at her from between narrowed lids.

Eva nodded abruptly as she stood up to slip the shirt off her shoulders and slide it off her arms before dropping it down onto the barstool. 'It's time that I left.'

'You have nothing else to say?' Markos could only stare at her with frustrated anger.

She looked up at him with eyes of deep, smoky amber. 'I've behaved badly, unprofessionally. Otherwise I don't know what else you want me to say.'

Markos wanted Eva to dismiss the lies Donna Cresswell had told her about him—to assure him that she had come to know him for herself this past week, and that she at least liked what she had come to know of him, that they had spent the day in bed together because of that liking.

The guarded expression in Eva's eyes told him that was never going to happen.

'Nothing,' he said flatly. 'Obviously there is nothing more you can or wish to say to me.'

She nodded abruptly. 'Which is why I am going to collect my bag from the bedroom and leave.'

Just an hour ago Markos had been filled with a feeling of well-being, of contentment in a woman's company and in lovemaking such as he had never experienced before. Only for all of those feelings to have been completely shattered by one telephone call.

He nodded abruptly. 'I will need to accompany you.'

'I'm perfectly capable of seeing myself out, Markos!' she assured him heavily.

His jaw tightened. 'The lift will not work without putting in my security code, and the same applies to the outside door.'

Colour darkened the pallor of her cheeks at the obvious rebuke. 'I'll just go and get my bag.'

Markos was filled with regret as he turned to watch Eva leave the kitchen—her back very straight and proud, her hips swaying slightly, sensuously, as she walked, her legs long and shapely in the high-heeled black sandals—but he knew he was too angry still to attempt to set things right between the two of them.

If such a thing was even possible...

Eva held back the tears for as long as it took her to reach Markos's bedroom, then she couldn't hold back her emotions any longer and instead allowed the tears to cascade down her cheeks with the heat of molten lava.

How could this be ending so badly?

How could she and Markos be parting like virtual strangers after having made love together so tenderly, and then so wildly, only hours ago?

The answer to that, Eva knew, lay firmly at her own door. Because she had too easily accepted Donna's telephone calls and her conversation as a link with her otherwise uncaring family rather than remembering her cousin as how she really was: a shallow social climber who had always had to have everything bigger and better than Eva.

She had been a fool, Eva accepted dully, a blind, stupid fool. There was absolutely no excuse for her initial scathing behaviour towards Markos. No foundation in it either—as she now knew.

Neither did it do any good now to tell herself that she should have looked beyond Donna's claims of Markos's mistreatment, should have seen Markos for the man he truly was—if not from the beginning then at least following his warmth and kindness towards her last night.

And now it was too late.

Yes, Markos was a man who was extremely attractive to women, and it was an attraction he had no doubt taken every advantage of over the years. But, as Eva now knew, he was also a man of principle. A man who had been both protective and caring when she had fallen apart at Jonathan's home the evening before following her introduction to the pregnant Yvette Cabot Grey. The same man who had allowed Eva to cry on his shoulder even though he had mistakenly believed those tears to have been because she still had feelings for her ex-husband. The same man who had brought her back to his apartment, put her in his own bed, undressing her and tucking her beneath the bedcovers.

The womanising Markos Lyonedes that Donna had led Eva to believe in wouldn't have bothered himself doing any of those things, let alone left her to sleep alone in his bed because he had no intention of taking advantage of her in her emotional state.

Eva hadn't just been a fool where Markos was concerned, she had been both blind and stupid too!

A realisation, an admission, which made absolutely no difference to the fact that she was now about to leave Markos's apartment and would in all probability never see him again.

But there was something she needed to say to him before she left…

'I'm sorry.'

Markos was standing in front of one of the huge picture windows in the sitting room, staring sightlessly out at the New York skyline, but he turned now to face Eva, his expression unreadable as he took in the fact that she was still very pale, and her eyes were that deep and troubled amber. As well they might be.

'What are you apologising for?' he returned impatiently.

She shrugged as she came further into the room, her gaze not quite meeting his as instead she stared at the centre of his chest. 'I— It's no excuse, but I—I was obviously misled about your involvement with Donna—or rather your lack of it,' she amended hastily as Markos's expression darkened.

'Yes?'

Her smile was rueful. 'You aren't about to make this easy for me, are you.'

He raised dark brows. 'Can you think of any reason why I should?'

'No,' she accepted heavily, before raising her chin and at last allowing her gaze to meet his. 'I do sincerely apologise for my earlier behaviour towards you. My lack of professionalism. I really should have known better than to believe Donna's lies.' She sighed. 'Or at the very least given you the benefit of the doubt—as you several times requested I might do,' she added.

'Yes, you should,' Markos bit out grimly.

She shifted her shoulders uncomfortably. 'I— And thank you for being so understanding yesterday evening. You really were very kind.'

'Maybe you believe there was an ulterior motive to my kindness and understanding?' Markos came back challengingly. 'After all, I did succeed in getting you into my bed—eventually!' He gave a derisive grimace. 'Which should fit in very nicely with what your cousin, the gossips and the newspapers have told you about me.' His mouth twisted scornfully.

Eva knew she deserved every ounce of that scorn, and that there was no way for her to salvage the situation without revealing how much her feelings towards him had changed. She might now know that Markos *wasn't* the cold and callous bastard in regard to women and relationships that Donna had told her he was, but neither was he a man interested in an emotional relationship.

She nodded abruptly. 'I'll leave you now to enjoy the rest of your day. If you would like to do so, you can keep the designs and the swatches of material. Although another designer would probably prefer to—'

'There is not going to be another designer, Eva,' he cut in firmly.

Her eyes widened in surprise. 'You've decided not to bother after all...?'

'On the contrary,' Markos drawled dryly, 'I have decided to keep the interior designer I already have.'

She blinked, long dark lashes briefly brushing against the pallor of her cheeks. 'I'm not sure I understand...?'

'It's quite simple, Eva.' Markos strode into the middle of the room. 'I have already wasted a considerable amount of my time procuring the services of the elusive but celebrated designer Evangeline Grey.' He eyed her mockingly. 'And, having done so, I have no intention of starting the process all over again.'

Eva eyed him warily even as she chewed distractedly on her bottom lip. 'You still want to engage me to redesign your apartment?'

His eyes glittered deeply emerald. 'I don't just want you to do it, Eva, I *insist* upon it!'

And if that determined glitter in his eyes was any

indication then Eva knew he intended making her life very uncomfortable—even more uncomfortable than it already was—while she did it.

'Markos, you can't seriously want to have me hanging around here for the next few weeks—or months—after we… Well, you just can't,' she protested weakly once she had regained her breath enough to speak at all.

'On the contrary, I believe I would very much enjoy the experience,' he drawled mockingly.

Her heart sank at the implacability of his expression. 'Of watching me squirm with embarrassment every time I have to come here?'

Markos shrugged those broad, uncompromising shoulders. 'If that's what it takes, yes.'

This was a side of him that Eva had never seen before. The arrogantly powerful Markos Lyonedes side of him—Greek, half-owner of the world-renowned company Lyonedes Enterprises, cousin of the equally arrogant and powerful Drakon Lyonedes, and a man accustomed to issuing orders and expecting them to be obeyed. Without question or argument.

Until he had actually made that statement Markos had had no idea he had even decided on that particular course of action. But it did make perfect sense; Eva had already done all the groundwork towards redesigning this room at least, and he had no doubt she would be as successful in her designs for the rest of the apartment.

Besides which, he hadn't decided yet exactly what he was going to do about Evangeline Grey.

Part of him definitely wanted to strangle her for having believed Donna Cresswell's lies about him, just as there was still a part of him that hungered to make love to her. And Markos had absolutely no idea which of those emotions was going to win once he had recovered from the disappointment he was currently feeling.

In the meantime, while he waited for those feelings to settle, it seemed like a good idea to keep Eva exactly where he could see her.

Even if his body *had* already made its decision, now engorged and throbbing in favour of taking Eva back to bed and making love to her until she had no strength with which to leave his bed…

'I will expect you to begin work on this room immediately,' he bit out abruptly. 'With the intention of presenting designs for the other rooms as soon as possible.'

'All of them?' Eva gasped.

'All of them,' Markos confirmed with satisfaction at her obvious dismay.

Leaving Eva in no doubt that Markos intended exacting his pound of flesh for her ever having harboured doubts as to his true nature.

She should never have allowed herself to jump to conclusions where Markos was concerned based only on what Donna had told her, or allowed those conclusions to influence her into behaving so badly, so unprofessionally, towards him at the beginning.

In truth, Eva now felt deeply ashamed of her behaviour. Something which wasn't going to be in the least alleviated during the telephone call she intended making to her duplicitous cousin as soon as she had reached the privacy of her apartment!

For now she just had to concentrate on leaving *this* apartment—leaving Markos—with at least some of her pride intact. 'If you're sure that's what you want…?'

'It is,' he rasped harshly.

'Fine.' Eva nodded briskly as she turned to leave.

'Oh, and, Eva…?'

'Yes?' She turned back warily.

'After, as you have so rightly called it, your lack of professionalism in regard to working for me, I will now expect you to give me your services exclusively for the next few weeks, at least.'

'That's imp—'

'And for you to inform me immediately if you have any further trouble with Cabot Grey,' he continued grimly.

'I don't consider *that* any of your business!' Eva gasped incredulously.

Markos's tread was light and predatory as he strode across the sitting room until he was standing only inches in front of her. 'After today I am *making* it my business.' His voice was dangerously soft. 'Do you understand, Eva?'

Oh, yes, she understood—only too well. And she resented the hell out of Markos's arrogant assumption that the two of them having made love together gave him any right to know anything about her private life.

Except it wasn't just a case of the two of them having made love together, was it? She had no idea what might have happened if Markos hadn't been with her last night when she'd realised Jack's second wife was pregnant—if he hadn't been so supportive of her in front of Jack and then later, here at his apartment.

'If I have any further trouble with Jack I will tell you about it,' she bit out tightly. 'Now can I leave?' she prompted angrily.

'Of course.' Markos smiled his satisfaction—both at Eva's reply and the fact that her fighting spirit had so obviously returned. He enjoyed verbally sparring with her almost as much as he had enjoyed making love with her. Almost…

'How kind of you!' Her eyes flashed deeply gold.

'In future, kindness is my middle name,' he drawled mockingly.

'And I thought it was arrogance,' she came back tartly.

Markos gave a husky chuckle. 'I will very much look forward to seeing you back here promptly at nine o'clock tomorrow morning.'

The fire dissipated from her eyes and she looked at him uncertainly. 'Markos—'

'Nine o'clock tomorrow morning, Eva,' he repeated firmly.

No matter how much Eva might wish it otherwise, Markos knew that things were far from settled between them…

CHAPTER ELEVEN

'So, what do you think…?' Eva looked at Markos uncertainly as he stood on the threshold of his newly decorated sitting room.

Markos thought that during the past three weeks he had learnt first-hand exactly what hell was!

It wore figure-hugging denims, form-fitting white T-shirts over full and luscious breasts, had long ebony hair, golden eyes, kissable lips, smelled of something lightly floral and sensual—and went under the guise of interior designer Evangeline Grey!

Because that was exactly who Eva had become during these three hellish weeks. Crisp, no-nonsense, utterly professional and bearing absolutely no resemblance to the woman Markos had made love with during that memorable Sunday.

The first week hadn't been too excruciating. Eva had only appeared at his apartment on the Monday and Tuesday, when she came in to take precise measurements for the carpets, curtains and other draperies.

The second week she had been more in evidence—calling in briefly every day in order to supervise her team of decorators, and to present Markos with the designs she had made for the rest of the rooms in his apartment.

And each time she'd arrived Markos had been the one who met her at the main lift before taking her up to his apartment.

By the time the furniture and fittings had arrived in the third week Markos had contacted Security and instructed them to let Eva in to the building any time she arrived, as well as giving her his security code to the private lift going straight up to his apartment.

All in an effort to spare himself the ordeal of so much as *seeing* the coolly remote stranger that Eva had become, let alone actually speaking to her.

And yet…any time Eva was in the building Markos instinctively knew she was up there—in his apartment, in the room just above his office.

He had been both angry and hurt the day he had insisted she would continue to redesign the interior of his apartment—and now he had found *he* was the one being punished, as day after day he was forced to suffer the cold professionalism of her manner towards him.

None of which was helped by the fact that every time he walked into his apartment his senses were bombarded with…well, with the presence of Eva.

He could see her influence now everywhere he looked in this newly furnished and decorated room: the pale terracotta-coloured walls adorned with bold coloured paintings of Greek islands, the carpet the colour of the Aegean Sea in summer, the deep rust colour of the comfortable sofas and chairs adorned with many scatter cushions in colours of blues and greens and yellows, the curtains draped at the huge picture windows in those same rich colours.

Such boldness of colour should have been too much, and yet somehow it not only worked but it also seemed to fill a hole in Markos's soul—a tiny oasis of need which was his love of Greece, a hunger that he hadn't even realised was there until he saw the colours and the warmth of his native country reflected so vividly in this room.

A hunger that Eva had not only seen and recognised in him, but addressed and filled with this warmth of colour…

He turned to her now. 'It's…amazing,' he said huskily.

'In a good way or a bad way?'

Markos gave a rueful smile as he recognised the wariness in Eva's tone. 'A good way, of course.' He stepped further into the room and allowed those warm Aegean colours to seep into his inner being, filling him with the same sense of peace and tranquillity he felt whenever he returned to Greece. Which was nowhere near as often as he would have liked it to be.

Eva heaved a deep sigh of relief as she felt the heavy weight of responsibility lift from her shoulders. She watched Markos's pleasure in his surroundings; as she had imagined, the richness and boldness of the earth tones suited Markos perfectly, bringing that same warm richness to his eyes and his swarthy, chiselled features as he strolled about the room.

She still couldn't believe she had been so stupid as to believe Donna's fantastic series of lies. Although, in her defence, she *had* started to doubt her cousin's version of things shortly after meeting Markos herself.

But she had only doubted Donna's version—she had never even thought that the whole thing had been a complete fabrication from start to finish. Nothing more than a figment of Donna's over-achieving imagination. Something, having spoken bluntly with Donna herself, Eva now knew without a shadow of a doubt to be the real truth.

Not that her cousin had apologised for the lies—in fact Donna appeared to be more angry towards Eva than anything else, for what she now saw as Eva's family disloyalty in befriending Markos herself.

Befriending?

Eva would hardly class the fantastic, earth-shattering lovemaking she and Markos had shared as 'befriending' each other!

God, just remembering the depth and feeling of that lovemaking now was enough to make her nipples tingle and tighten, to make her clench and unclench between her thighs.

She straightened abruptly. 'I'm pleased you're happy with it.'

'That would be an understatement.' Markos turned to look across at her from between narrowed lids. 'Praise where praise is due, Eva: you've done a fantastic job on this room.'

She avoided meeting that piercing gaze. 'Let's hope you're as pleased with the rest of the apartment once it's finished,' she dismissed briskly as she looked around for her shoulder bag.

'Perhaps we should have a glass of champagne to celebrate? Oh, come on, Eva,' he drawled dryly as she turned to him with wide eyes. 'I can't be the first satisfied customer who has wanted to toast the success of your hard work?'

He was the first satisfied customer that Eva had gone to bed with.

The only man, besides Jack, she had *ever* been to bed with...

And Eva now knew beyond a shadow of a doubt that there was absolutely no comparison between the two men. Jack had been a selfish lover, whereas Markos was a generous one. She had been a virgin when she'd married Jack, had had no idea that making love should be the way it had been between her and Markos—a delight for all the senses.

And those memories weren't helping her in the least to keep this meeting on a business footing! 'I really do have to go—'

'Do you have a date this evening?'

'No, of course not,' she answered with irritation.

'Have you heard from Cabot Grey?'

Eva drew her breath in sharply. 'I've spoken to Jack again, yes,' she confirmed guardedly.

Markos looked at her from between narrowed lids, having absolutely no idea what thoughts were going on behind those shuttered gold-coloured eyes. 'I believe I asked you to tell me—'

'If I had any further trouble from Jack. Which I haven't,' she added firmly. 'We spoke. Nothing more.'

'About what?'

She gave a pained frown. 'As I've said before, I don't believe that to be any of your business—'

'That's bull—' He abruptly broke off his angry response, aware that he had been about to voice an unacceptable expletive. His jaw was tight as he continued between gritted teeth, 'As the man who helped you to pick up the pieces after your last conversation with your ex-husband, I happen to think it's very *much* my business!' His eyes glittered darkly.

A blush heightened Eva's cheeks. 'I believe I've already thanked you sufficiently for the…assistance you gave me that weekend.'

'I sincerely hope that was *not* a reference to our love-making, Eva,' he bit out coldly.

'Of course not!' she gasped.

'No?'

She gave another pained wince. 'Markos, I've already thanked you several times for your kindness the evening I met Jack again at his father's house. And it's because of that kindness that I refuse to argue with you now—'

'Then what *are* you going to do with me?'

She blinked. 'Sorry?'

'Not half as sorry as I am!' Markos muttered grimly under his breath. He spoke more loudly. 'I asked what are you going to do about me, Eva?'

She gave a puzzled shake of her head. 'I'm sorry, but I still don't understand what you mean…'

No, Markos could see by the blankness of Eva's expression that she really didn't understand—that as far as she was concerned theirs was now a purely business relationship.

Which was exactly what Markos had implied it was going to be three weeks ago. Before he had been forced to live every day in this living hell of wanting Eva, of being driven quietly but surely out of his mind with the knowledge of that desire for her, while she obviously had had absolutely no difficulty in resuming their previous business relationship, shutting out all memory of their hours of intimacy.

Or perhaps she hadn't shut them out at all? Maybe she really had just forgotten them altogether?

It was an idea Markos found totally unacceptable.

He gave a shake of his head. 'Is this what you do, Eva? Is this what your marriage to Cabot Grey did to you? Did you have a couple of dates with Glen too, a night in bed together, and then not only discard him as unimportant but forget about him altogether?'

'Of course not,' she gasped tremulously, her eyes now amber pools of hurt. 'That really isn't fair, Markos. You not only flirted with me outrageously the evening we met, but once you realised who I was you also ensured I had no choice but to come here for our appointment on the Monday evening. If anyone forgot about Glen, discarded him, then it was *you*!'

His mouth twisted derisively. 'Have you seen him again since that evening?'

'No,' she breathed shakily.

'Why not?'

Eva flinched at the coldness in Markos's tone. At the subject of this whole conversation. 'How can you even *ask* me that?'

Markos raised mocking brows. His inner frustrations this past three weeks was making him determined to get some sort of response from Eva. Even if it was a negative one. 'Because if you haven't been seeing me, and you haven't been seeing Glen, then I'm interested to know who it is you're hurrying off to meet this evening. Your ex-husband, perhaps?'

'Don't be ridiculous!' Her face had paled to the colour of delicate white porcelain.

'Is *that* what I'm being?' Markos grated tautly.

'Where Jack is concerned, yes! Markos, you were there—you saw my reaction to seeing Jack again.'

'I saw your reaction to seeing his pregnant wife,' he corrected harshly. 'Which isn't the same thing at all.'

No, it wasn't, Eva acknowledged heavily. Not the same thing at all.

Jack had called her, as his parting comment that evening about 'being in touch' had promised that he would, and the two of them had agreed to meet in a suitably neutral coffee shop. The conversation had been stilted and awkward, but once Eva had convinced Jack that she had absolutely no interest in telling anyone that Yvette's baby couldn't be his the two of them had reached an uneasy truce, with an agreement that they would both stay out of the other's life, and if they met again socially would at least be polite to each other. Nothing more, but nothing less, either.

It wasn't perfect, but it was far better than the anger which had burned so strongly between them before Eva had realised she was allowing her life to be ruined because of her failed marriage.

It was a realisation which had made her determined to put that part of her life behind her and move on to whatever kind of future might be in store for her, rather than the future she had so neatly planned out for herself.

In a perfect world Eva knew that future would have included Markos—the man she had come to realise these past three weeks she was so very much in love with...

Not that bedazzled young love she had felt for Jack, but the love of a mature woman who knew what and who she was, and also knew how and who she loved.

Eva had no idea how or when it had happened. Perhaps when Markos had defended her so gallantly in front of Jack. Or perhaps it had been the gentleness of his care when he'd rescued her from the bathroom and taken her back to his apartment, before undressing her and leaving her to sleep alone in his bed. Or during that wild and glorious lovemaking the following day, the memory of which still caused Eva to tremble just thinking about it.

Or maybe, just maybe, it had happened the first moment she'd set eyes on him at Senator Ashcroft's cocktail party...

It didn't really matter when or how it had happened, only that it had. She was in love with Markos Lyonedes. Completely. Utterly. And he was obviously still as disgusted with her as he had been three weeks ago.

She gave a weary sigh, accepting that perhaps she *did* owe Markos at least some answers to his questions. 'I did meet Jack again after his father's party—'

'You *met* him?' Markos echoed incredulously. 'He's a married man, about to become a father, and the two of you still sneaked away together behind his wife's back—'

'It wasn't like that!' Eva protested painfully.

'No?' The look Markos gave her down the long length of his aristocratic nose spoke of his disgust. 'Then tell me what it *was* like, Eva.'

Eva had absolutely no doubt that this past three weeks—with the two of them skirting around each other, being outwardly polite and inwardly a seething mass of emotions and unanswered questions—had been leading up to this confrontation. A confrontation she had no idea whether or not she was ready for, but she accepted it was coming anyway.

'Did Jack tell Yvette about your meeting?' Markos pressured.

'I have no idea,' she answered honestly. 'He may have done. There's no reason why he shouldn't have.'

Markos gave a disgusted snort. 'I can think of plenty of reasons a man wouldn't tell his heavily pregnant second wife that he was going off to meet his first wife!'

'I said it wasn't like that!' Eva glared at Markos. 'Jack and I had…unresolved issues we needed to talk about—no, damn it, *not* those sort of issues!' she snapped angrily when she saw how the censure in Markos's eyes had deepened. 'There was so much anger between us still when we parted and divorced. I had wanted a baby so much, and Jack— He refused even to consider adoption, and he was totally against the idea of IVF with another man's donated sperm. It caused a huge rift and we drifted apart. He began to have affairs—'

'Just a minute.' Markos's voice was husky as he halted her, 'I thought you told me that you were the one who couldn't have children.'

A frown creased her creamy brow as she slowly shook her head. 'I couldn't have said that because it isn't true.'

No, she *hadn't* exactly said that, Markos realised, slightly dazed.

What Eva had said was that she and Jack had had tests, and that it wasn't possible for them to have a child together. *He* had made the assumption that night, because of Eva's distress, that she was the one incapable of having a child of her own.

Markos frowned darkly. 'But if Cabot Grey is sterile, then how are he and Yvette—?'

'Don't ask.' Eva gave a weary shake of her head. 'As far as the world is concerned—and, more importantly, Jonathan Cabot Grey Senior—the baby Yvette is expecting is Jack's son and heir. And I think it's best for all concerned if it remains that way.'

Markos felt short of breath—as if someone had punched him hard in the chest. Damn it, he hadn't used contraception when the two of them made love because he had believed a pregnancy was impossible! 'So you *are* able to have children?'

'Yes,' she confirmed flatly. 'In fact I— Look, as our conversation has gone this far, I might as well be completely honest with you.'

'That would certainly be a novelty!' He looked at her coldly.

Her eyes flashed deeply golden. 'I have *never* been dishonest with you!'

'Except by omission.'

'Perhaps,' she acknowledged heavily, her gaze no longer quite meeting his. 'The truth is I decided some months ago to have a child of my own by IVF.'

Markos's thoughts were already reeling from one realisation to another, one question to another, and each one was becoming wilder than the last. Eva *could* have a baby, after all. In fact it now appeared she had coolly and calmly decided to do exactly that 'some months ago'...

His gaze sharpened. 'And can it be that you were considering the blue-eyed blond-haired Glen Asher as a possible candidate to be the donor for this IVF?'

The warmth of colour entered the paleness of Eva's cheeks. 'I considered it, yes.'

'And did he agree?' Markos grated harshly, feeling a fury building up inside him the like of which he had never experienced before.

Eva's smile was completely lacking in humour. 'We didn't get far enough in our friendship for me to broach such a sensitive subject as IVF with him.'

Markos gave a disgusted shake of his head. 'Why not just forget the whole idea of IVF and instead just go to bed with him and hope for the desired result? He would certainly have been willing!'

Her throat moved convulsively as she swallowed before speaking. 'After my marriage to Jack I didn't want the trauma of being intimately involved again. Nor did I want the complication of having my child's life ripped apart by estranged parents, and so I thought—I thought a legal contract with a sperm donor, followed by IVF—'

'It seems to me, with all your talk of "I didn't want" and "nor did I want", that you weren't thinking of anything or anyone but yourself, Eva,' Markos cut in coldly.

No, she hadn't, Eva acknowledged numbly. The woman she had been—cool and businesslike, and determined not to become physically involved with any man—had made her decision to have a baby without emotion, without any real thought for the emotional consequences of those actions.

The woman she had been...

Eva knew she was no longer that hurt and disillusioned woman. She had ceased being that woman even before she and Markos had made love together. She had become another woman completely when she'd fallen in love with him...

It was a love which she knew, just from looking at the disgust now on Markos's face when he looked at her, was even more doomed than her marriage to Jack had been.

'Did you seriously think that Glen Asher—that *any* man,' Markos continued disgustedly, 'would just calmly agree to cold-bloodedly, cold-heartedly donate his sperm for you to be impregnated with?'

She moved agitatedly. 'As you've just pointed out, I don't believe I had been thinking straight for some time.'

She didn't particularly care for the way Markos was now looking at her from between narrowed lids, as if she were a specimen under a microscope—a hitherto unknown species he was trying, and not succeeding, to understand. And what little he *did* understand he didn't particularly like.

'You could be pregnant now, Eva.'

'What…?'

His mouth was a thin straight line. 'Three weeks ago I believed, from our previous conversation, that you were incapable of becoming pregnant, rendering precautions unnecessary when we made love together. Did you take any steps yourself to prevent a pregnancy?'

Eva stared at him uncomprehendingly. No, of course she hadn't. There had never been any reason for her to. She had known she couldn't become pregnant during her marriage, and there had been no other man intimately in her life since her divorce, so there had never been any need for the use of any sort of contraception.

Markos had now been intimately in her life—however briefly. Several times.

'Are you pregnant, Eva?' Markos repeated harshly.

Was she? Eva desperately tried to recall when she had last had a period and failed utterly, her mind having gone a complete blank.

Of *course* she wasn't pregnant!

Was she...?

Markos didn't feel in the least encouraged by the way Eva's face had turned a sickly grey colour. As if she were fighting down nausea.

Nausea possibly caused by early pregnancy...

The irony of this situation wasn't lost on Markos. Eva's cousin, and other ambitious women like her, would, he knew, quite happily become pregnant as a way of entrapping a wealthy man into marriage. Typically Eva—contrarily so!—she had decided to become pregnant by totally eliminating any physical intimacy or personal knowledge of the man who had made her so!

Unfortunately for Eva that was never going to happen if it turned out she was now carrying his child.

'Well?' he prompted tersely.

Eva determinedly gathered her scattered thoughts together, knowing this was neither the time nor the place for her to dwell on the chaos of her own thoughts. 'I can't believe you're so full of yourself, Markos, that you actually believe yourself to be so virile a woman would become pregnant from just one day of unprotected sex with you!' she added mockingly.

The coldness in those deep emerald eyes deepened. 'One day during which we indulged in several occasions of unprotected sex,' he corrected harshly.

She gave an unconcerned shrug. 'Well, I'm sorry to

disappoint you, Markos, but I guess you really aren't as potent as you thought you were.'

Was that disappointment he was feeling? Markos wondered scowlingly. Or did he feel disappointment because he had realised, with the flatness of Eva's denial of pregnancy, that their relationship—friendship—whatever—had now to come to an end?

There had been too much said for the two of them to carry on with even their business arrangement as if nothing had happened.

'Damn it!' Markos cursed. 'Why do you have to be so damned complicated?'

She gave a wistful smile. 'Just unlucky for you, I guess.'

Markos thought back to the first time he had seen Eva at Senator Ashcroft's drinks party, to his instant awareness of her, his instant attraction to the voluptuously beautiful woman in the red gown who'd drawn him towards her like a magnet. *Then* the situation had been uncomplicated. *Then* she had just been a lushly beautiful woman in a red gown that he had wanted to make love to.

Markos had never done complicated. A woman either was or was not interested in a brief and meaningless affair. He had never had the time or the inclination for anything more than that.

'Am I allowed to leave now?'

Markos's mouth tightened and he looked up to find himself the focus of beautiful gold-coloured eyes that danced with bittersweet laughter.

'I'm glad one of us finds this situation amusing!'

Eva wasn't in the least amused at the idea of never seeing Markos again, but it was better than crying.

She had already broken down emotionally enough in Markos's company. She certainly didn't intend to let him see her doing it now because she knew, despite everything, that she was in love with him. That would just be too humiliating.

She drew in a deep breath. 'Can I take it that you would now be happier if another interior designer took over refurbishing the rest of your apartment?'

A nerve pulsed in his tightly clenched jaw. 'You can.'

'That's what I thought.' Eva nodded abruptly. 'Well, it's been…interesting meeting you, Markos.' She slung her bag over her shoulder in preparation for leaving.

'Don't forget to send me the bill for the work you've already done,' he reminded her flatly.

'And don't *you* forget to change the security code on your private lift,' she said lightly.

He arched one dark and mocking brow. 'Is there any danger of your ever wanting to come back here?'

'Probably not,' she acknowledged with a tight smile.

'Then why would I bother changing the security code?' He shrugged unconcernedly.

Eva hesitated. 'I'm sure you're not really interested, but I—I've now decided not to go ahead with my plans for IVF.'

A nerve pulsed in his jaw. 'Why not?'

She gave a wistful smile, knowing she couldn't tell Markos the real reason—that, having fallen in love with him, it was impossible for her ever to want anyone else's child but his. 'Maybe I'm no longer that selfish.'

'I was wrong to say that,' Markos spoke huskily. 'After what you went through during your marriage to Cabot Grey it was not selfish to want a child of your own, Eva.'

'Merely ill-advised?' She grimaced.

'Not that either.' He gave a slow shake of his head.

'Then what was it?'

'I have absolutely no idea,' he admitted evenly.

She nodded abruptly. 'Goodbye, Markos.'

'Eva,' he returned tersely.

She wouldn't cry, Eva told herself firmly as she walked over to step inside the waiting lift before turning to look across at Markos where he stood so tall and darkly handsome—and icily distant—across the room.

She would *not* cry.

She had loved and lost, yes, but she had no one to blame for that but herself.

It was a loss Eva had a feeling she was going to have to live with for the rest of her life…

CHAPTER TWELVE

Eva paced restlessly up and down her apartment the following morning, checking her watch constantly as she waited—and waited!—for what might be considered a reasonable time to telephone someone—to telephone Markos!—on a Saturday morning.

Seven a.m.

Seven-fifteen.

Seven-thirty.

Seven forty-five.

And each of those minutes seemed like an hour as the second hand on Eva's watch crawled round more slowly with every second, increasing her tension. Those minutes had been crawling round all night as Eva had felt too restless even to go to bed, let alone try to sleep.

Eight a.m.

Eight fifteen.

Eight-thirty.

Was eight thirty still too early to telephone Markos? Would he still be in—?

Eva's nerves were strung out so tightly that she jumped about two feet in the air as the tune of her mobile ringing broke shrilly into the silence. She took several seconds to settle her jitteriness before picking up the phone, distractedly noting that the caller ID was 'unknown' and hoping whoever it was would get off the line quickly, so that she could put her own call through to Markos. Before she lost her nerve.

'Evangeline Grey,' she answered briskly.

'Eva.'

Just her name. Just that one word. And yet Eva knew without a shadow of a doubt that the person on the other end of the line was Markos.

'How strange, Markos, I was just about to call you…' she told him huskily.

'You were?'

She could hear the surprise in his tone. 'I need to talk to you.'

'You do?'

Eva gave a slightly breathless laugh as Markos also continued to sound less than his usually arrogantly confident self. 'Yes, I do. Is it convenient for me to come over now?'

'Not necessary. I'm already in the car on my way over to see you,' he came back dryly.

Now it was Eva's turn to feel surprised, and her fingers tightened about the mobile, the inside of her mouth having gone suddenly dry.

'You are?'

'I am,' he assured her firmly—*grimly*? 'I should reach your apartment in fifteen minutes or so, traffic allowing.'

She heaved a shakily relieved sigh, longing to see him again, to speak with him. 'Markos—'

'I would rather we talked face to face, Eva,' he cut in determinedly.

'Okay.' It was what she wanted too. 'I'll tell Security

to expect you.' She moistened her lips. 'Drive carefully,' she added huskily.

'Depend on it.' Markos abruptly ended the call.

Eva switched off her mobile before replacing it carefully back on the coffee table, hardly daring to believe that Markos wanted to speak to her—that he was actually on his way to her apartment right now.

She had spent hours the previous night, pacing from room to room in her apartment as she tried to decide what to do for the best. Talk to Markos. Don't talk to him. And in the end it had all come back to the realisation that she *had* to talk to him.

Did the fact that Markos seemed to have decided the same thing, in regard to her, make what she had to say to him easier or harder?

No doubt in fifteen minutes or so Eva would have the answer to that question. And several more.

'I brought coffee…' Markos held up a cardboard tray holding two take-away coffees when Eva opened her apartment door to him fifteen minutes later. 'The "hot" young man who works in the coffee shop across the road on weekends assured me this is how you take your coffee,' he added dryly.

Eva felt warmth in her cheeks as she remembered that deliberately provocative conversation. On her part at least.

'You told him it was for me…?'

Markos arched mocking brows. 'I only had to mention that you lived in this particular apartment building and he knew exactly who you were, and how you take your coffee. So much for him not noticing you, hmm?' he added teasingly as Eva tacitly invited him into her apartment by opening the door wider and stepping aside.

Her apartment seemed much smaller once Markos was inside, Eva noted—his very presence, in faded denims and a casual black shirt unbuttoned at the throat, with the sleeves turned up to just below his elbows, seemed to dominate even the air she breathed in so shallowly as she entered the sitting room behind him.

'This is beautiful.' Markos placed the cardboard tray down on the coffee table as he looked about the comfort of Eva's sitting room. The décor was in autumn colours—reds, golds, oranges, and all shades in between—and a perfect foil for her dark-haired golden-eyed beauty. 'It suits you.'

Eva's face was a little pale this morning, but otherwise she looked as arrestingly beautiful as usual, in fitted black denims and a pale lemon T-shirt.

'Here.' Markos picked up the coffee he had brought for her and held it out to her. 'You look as if you need it,' he added.

Her hand shook slightly as she took the insulated cup from him. 'And then we'll talk?' She smiled warily.

'And then we'll talk,' Markos confirmed, frowning as he once again noted the fragility of Eva's appearance.

He had spent a restless evening and a sleepless night after Eva had left his apartment the evening before, as he'd tried to accept that they were never going to see each other again. He had spent hours going over and over everything they had said during that last conversation, ultimately coming to the conclusion that none of it was of the least consequence when all he wanted was to see Eva again. To be with her. Once Markos had accepted that truth, everything else had become unimportant.

Convincing Eva to feel the same way about him might take a little longer!

'Markos...?' Eva had no idea what thoughts were currently going through Markos's head—when had she *ever* known what this enigmatic man was really thinking?—but whatever they were, they were causing him to frown darkly.

He shook off that darkness as he straightened. 'You said you wanted to speak to me this morning...?'

She moistened her lips before speaking. 'I believe we admitted we wanted to speak to each other?'

He gave a derisive smile. 'I'm really not in the mood to play games today, Eva.'

'Me either,' she assured him.

This situation, the conversation they needed to have, was too important for that.

'Which one of us should go first?'

Markos was tired—not only from his lack of sleep the night before, but by the way the two of them seemed to be skirting so warily around each other this morning.

'Will you marry me, Eva?'

'*What?*' she managed to burst out, eyes wide and disbelieving, her cheeks paling even more before colouring with a deep flush.

Not the most encouraging reaction to his first marriage proposal—the only marriage proposal Markos intended ever making. If Eva didn't accept him, then he couldn't see himself ever wanting to be with anyone else.

'I asked if you would become my wife,' he replied. 'Don't turn it down without due consideration,' he added quickly, when Eva seemed to be searching for the right words in answer to his proposal. No doubt a refusal that she hoped would cause the least embarrassment for both of them.

'Are you serious?' she finally managed to ask.

He nodded tersely. 'Think about it, Eva. I'm very wealthy. Socially acceptable—'

'I've already been married to someone with those particular attributes,' she reminded him huskily. 'It was a disaster!'

'I have no reason to believe I'm infertile,' Markos continued firmly. 'Although I'm willing to have the necessary tests to prove it, if that is what it takes to convince you to marry me.' He grimaced. 'Once we are married you can have as many babies as you want. One a year if you want to— Eva…?' he prompted sharply as she sat down abruptly in one of the armchairs and buried her face in her hands. 'Eva!' He went down on his haunches beside her chair. 'Do not cry, my Eva,' he pleaded. 'I hate it when you cry.'

Eva didn't doubt that for a moment. She could hear the distress in Markos's voice, and the way his accent became more pronounced whenever he was disturbed or upset.

But what he had just said was so unexpected, so totally beyond the realms of what she had expected him to say, that she couldn't quite take it in.

'I'm not crying, Markos.' She gave a firm shake of her head and took her hands from in front of her face to look up at him, crouching down only inches in front of her, his expression anxious. 'I was laughing.'

'Laughing?' he repeated incredulously as he surged abruptly to his feet. 'I propose marriage and you *laugh*!'

He scowled darkly. 'Is the idea of marrying me so amusing, then?'

Eva sobered completely when she saw Markos's hurt reflected in those deep green eyes. 'No, of course it isn't. I just— It was— I didn't expect—'

'For me to propose to you?' he guessed. 'If it is any consolation, it was the last thing I expected of myself when I made this move to New York just a matter of weeks ago!'

Yes, Eva could imagine it was. She doubted that Markos had seen himself married to anyone, in his near future.

'Why?' she prompted bluntly.

His brows rose. 'Why am I surprised? Or why did I propose to you?'

'The latter,' Eva replied dryly.

He shrugged broad shoulders. 'Why does any man propose marriage to a woman?' he came back defensively.

It was a defensive attitude that Eva knew was wholly merited when as far as Markos was concerned she had laughed at his proposal. 'Markos, I wasn't laughing at you just now, but at the irony of this situation,' she told him huskily. 'Did you mean what you said just now?'

'When I proposed—?'

'No, not that,' Eva cut in firmly.

'That if you married me we could have a dozen children together, if that is what you want? You really *are* about to cry now, Eva!' He groaned as he saw the tears well up in her eyes. 'I promise not to mention marriage to you again if this hysteria of emotions is the effect it has on you.'

'Markos.'

Just the husky softness of his name was enough to silence him as Eva rose determinedly to her feet, her cheeks looking hot and flushed, her eyes glowing brightly.

'Markos, I couldn't marry anyone who didn't love me in the way I'm in love with them.'

His breath caught in his throat. 'You—'

'In the way I'm in love with *you*…'

Markos became very still, his eyes a deep and glowing emerald as he stared at her incredulously. 'You *love* me…?'

'So very much,' she breathed determinedly.

Markos blinked. 'And after you left me yesterday I realised, at the thought of not seeing you again, how very much in love with *you* I am—which is why I—'

'Will you marry me?'

He gave a dazed shake of his head. 'I do not understand. You seemed amused just now by my own marriage proposal, and now you are asking—'

'Will you wait here a moment?' she asked excitedly, before turning to leave.

'Where are you going?' Markos called after her incredulously.

'Eva, you cannot tell me you love me, allow me to tell you I love you, ask me to marry you, and then just leave the room—'

She turned. 'I have something I want to show you.'

'Eva, now is *not* the time for me to look at more of your designs for my apartment!' he told her exasperatedly, and he crossed the room in long determined strides, before taking a firm hold of the tops of her arms as he looked down at her intently. 'I love you, Eva. I am insane with love for you. I can think of nothing else, see nothing else, but *you*!'

'I love you in exactly the same way, Markos,' she assured him huskily, reaching up tenderly to cup the side of his face with her hand as she looked at him with that love glowing in her eyes. 'I've known how I feel about you for some weeks now—'

'How many weeks?'

Her lashes lowered at his continued incredulity. 'Almost from the beginning, I think...'

'From the beginning?' Markos's fingers tightened about her arms even as the love he felt for this beautiful, wonderful woman welled up strongly inside him. 'The night we met at Senator Ashcroft's drinks party?'

'Well, perhaps not quite then.' She looked up, her eyes alive with amusement. 'Admittedly Donna's lies didn't help the situation, but I was still feeling more than a little jaundiced about the whole idea of love and marriage then. So it came as something of a surprise to me when I found myself attracted to you anyway,' she acknowledged ruefully. 'When I continued to fall for you a little bit more each time we met.' She gazed steadily into his eyes. 'I believe I fell all the way in love with you after we went to Jonathan's party and you were so protective and caring of me.'

'Before or after we made love?' he teased gruffly.

'Oh, definitely before,' Eva answered him without hesitation. 'Markos, there has never been anyone else for me. Not before I was married. Or in the three years since. And I don't believe I would have made love with you that day if I hadn't already been in love with you.'

'And now?'

'Now I love you so much that I just want to be with

you all the time,' she admitted softly. 'With or without marriage.'

'And I will settle for nothing less than to be married to you for the rest of our lives,' Markos told her firmly.

'Does that mean you accept my marriage proposal?'

Markos felt the last of his tension leaving him as he grinned down at her. 'On the understanding that you realise after accepting I will then tease you mercilessly for the next fifty years about your having been the one who proposed!'

'I would expect nothing less,' she assured him unconcernedly.

Markos gave a triumphant laugh as he drew her fully into his arms and hugged her tightly against him. 'I love you so very much, Evangeline Grey-soon-to-be-Lyonedes!' he murmured huskily, and at last he claimed her mouth with his own.

It was a long, long time later before Eva remembered she had something else she wanted to tell Markos, to show him. The intensity and wonder of their lovemaking had wiped everything else from her mind but Markos and the joy of being in his arms.

She looked at him almost shyly as he lay back against the pillows in her bed, holding her cradled tenderly against him in the aftermath of that lovemaking.

'Markos, I have an early wedding present I would like to give you.'

He looked down at her indulgently, all the strain and tension now erased from his wonderfully handsome face. 'I have no need of anything else but the love you feel for me, my darling Eva, and the love I feel for you, and the long and happy life we are going to have together,' he assured her emphatically.

Eva sat up beside him to kiss him lingeringly on the lips before straightening. 'I'm hoping that you'll love the gift I'm about to give you just as much.'

Markos reached out to grasp one of her hands in his as she would have risen from the bed. 'Believe me when I tell you I could never love anything or anyone as much as I love you, my Eva.'

Her eyes glowed deeply golden with the love she felt for him. 'Wait and see...'

Markos lay back against the pillows, feeling his desire returning as he watched Eva get up and leave the bedroom, knowing that he would always feel this way about her.

It had been an agonisingly long and sleepness night after he and Eva had parted so badly the evening before. A long and restless night during which Markos had realised that in just a few short weeks Eva had not only taken possession of his heart but become the centre of his world, that he loved her, would always love her, more than life itself.

To be here with her now and know that she loved him in exactly the same way was joy beyond imagining.

'Here.'

Markos looked up uncomprehendingly as Eva sat down beside him on the bed, holding out what looked like a thermometer. 'I do not understand—'

'It's blue, Markos!' She glowed at him, looking heartbreakingly beautiful with her cheeks flushed and her eyes fever-bright.

He gave a puzzled shake of his head. 'What—?'

'We're pregnant, Markos!' She smiled widely, joy-

ously. 'I hadn't even considered the possibility until
you mentioned it last night. But once I did I stopped
off at a pharmacy on the way home and bought one
of these instant pregnancy kits. It's positive, Markos.
We're *pregnant*!' she said again excitedly. 'I think I was
in shock last night, once I'd found out, and by the time
I recovered I thought it was too late to call you. And
then the hours seemed to go by so slowly until I felt
it was late enough to call you this morning—but then
you called me instead, and— Markos…?' The flow of
words came to a halting stop as she realised he hadn't
yet said a word in response to her announcement.

Markos was in shock. He felt as if his heart had
stopped beating, that no air could enter his lungs.
His whole world had tilted on its axis before tilting
back again, leaving himself, Eva and the baby—*their*
baby!—having miraculously taken up residence in her
gloriously beautiful body. Not only did he have Eva's
love, but the two of them were going to have a baby
together.

The important word being *together*…

'You're going to be a father, Markos,' Eva told him
excitedly, still hardly able to believe the wonder of it
all herself.

All those years of trying to have a baby, of longing
for a baby, and when it had finally happened she hadn't
had a clue until Markos had put forward the possibility of it yesterday.

Her initial shock the evening before had quickly
been followed by a feeling of absolute awe. She was
pregnant at last. Nestled safe inside her was the baby of
the man Eva loved so much she ached with the emotion.

'That's why I was going to call you this morning. I

couldn't wait to share the wonderful news with you.' Her excitement wavered slightly as she looked down at Markos uncertainly. 'Markos, please say something, my darling...'

He sat up to take her gently in his arms. 'Thank you, my Eva,' he murmured gruffly into the silkiness of her hair.

'You're pleased about the baby?'

Markos pulled back slightly when he heard the uncertainty in Eva's voice, his hands moving up to cradle each side of her face. 'I am ecstatic about the baby,' he assured her firmly.

The way in which Eva had told him the news—the way in which she had said, 'We're pregnant, Markos!'— not *I'm* pregnant, but *we're* pregnant—and that he was going to be a father—dear Lord, the wonder of such a thing! It told Markos more than anything else ever could have done that those plans Eva had once had to have a baby on her own, without the complication of a man in either her bed or the life of her baby, no longer existed. She had wanted to share their baby with him from the moment she knew of its existence.

'I love you, Eva. I will always love you!' His arms tightened about her with a possessiveness he hadn't known he was capable of feeling until this moment of holding Eva and their baby in his arms.

Eva was his.

As Markos was hers.

And the baby she carried was and always would be theirs to share, and love, and nurture...

Together.

* * * * *

COMING NEXT MONTH from Harlequin Presents®
AVAILABLE AUGUST 21, 2012

#3083 CONTRACT WITH CONSEQUENCES
Miranda Lee
Scarlet wants a baby, but ruthless John Mitchell's help comes with a devilish price—that they do it the old-fashioned way!

#3084 DEFYING THE PRINCE
The Santina Crown
Sarah Morgan
Scandalized singer Izzy Jackson is whisked away from the baying press by Prince Matteo...straight from the limelight into the fire....

#3085 TO LOVE, HONOR AND BETRAY
Jennie Lucas
Callie never imagined that on her wedding day she would be kidnapped by her boss, Eduardo Cruz—the father of her unborn baby.

#3086 ENEMIES AT THE ALTAR
The Outrageous Sisters
Melanie Milburne
Sienna Baker is the last woman Andreas Ferrante would ever marry. But now she's the key to his inheritance!

#3087 DUTY AND THE BEAST
Desert Brothers
Trish Morey
Princess Aisha is rescued from the clutches of a lascivious prince by barbarian Zoltan. Now he must marry Aisha to ensure he's crowned king.

#3088 A TAINTED BEAUTY
What His Money Can't Buy
Sharon Kendrick
Ciro D'Angelo discovers his "perfect wife" isn't as pure as he'd thought! Yet once you're a D'Angelo wife—there's no escape....

You can find more information on upcoming Harlequin®
titles, free excerpts and more at www.Harlequin.com.

HPCNM0812

COMING NEXT MONTH from Harlequin Presents® EXTRA
AVAILABLE SEPTEMBER 4, 2012

#213 GIANNI'S PRIDE
Protecting His Legacy
Kim Lawrence
Can Gianni conquer his pride and admit that he might have met his match in utterly gorgeous Miranda?

#214 THE SECRET SINCLAIR
Protecting His Legacy
Cathy Williams
One spectacular night under Raoul's skilful touch leads to consequences Sarah could never have imagined: she's pregnant with the Sinclair heir!

#215 WHAT HAPPENS IN VEGAS...
Inconveniently Wed!
Kimberly Lang
Evie's scandalous baby bombshell will provide tantalising gossip-column fodder, unless she marries the dangerously attractive billionaire Nick Rocco...father of her baby!

#216 MARRYING THE ENEMY
Inconveniently Wed!
Nicola Marsh
Ruby finds herself propositioning tycoon Jax Maroney in order to save her family's company—but it's only a marriage on paper...isn't it?

REQUEST YOUR FREE BOOKS!

2 FREE NOVELS PLUS
2 FREE GIFTS!

YES! Please send me 2 FREE Harlequin Presents® novels and my 2 FREE gifts (gifts are worth about $10). After receiving them, if I don't wish to receive any more books, I can return the shipping statement marked "cancel." If I don't cancel, I will receive 6 brand-new novels every month and be billed just $4.30 per book in the U.S. or $4.99 per book in Canada. That's a saving of at least 14% off the cover price! It's quite a bargain! Shipping and handling is just 50¢ per book in the U.S. and 75¢ per book in Canada.* I understand that accepting the 2 free books and gifts places me under no obligation to buy anything. I can always return a shipment and cancel at any time. Even if I never buy another book, the two free books and gifts are mine to keep forever.

106/306 HDN FERQ

Name _____ (PLEASE PRINT) _____

Address _____ Apt. #

City _____ State/Prov. _____ Zip/Postal Code

Signature (if under 18, a parent or guardian must sign)

Mail to the **Reader Service:**
IN U.S.A.: P.O. Box 1867, Buffalo, NY 14240-1867
IN CANADA: P.O. Box 609, Fort Erie, Ontario L2A 5X3

Not valid for current subscribers to Harlequin Presents books.

**Are you a current subscriber to Harlequin Presents books
and want to receive the larger-print edition?
Call 1-800-873-8635 or visit www.ReaderService.com.**

* Terms and prices subject to change without notice. Prices do not include applicable taxes. Sales tax applicable in N.Y. Canadian residents will be charged applicable taxes. Offer not valid in Quebec. This offer is limited to one order per household. All orders subject to credit approval. Credit or debit balances in a customer's account(s) may be offset by any other outstanding balance owed by or to the customer. Please allow 4 to 6 weeks for delivery. Offer available while quantities last.

Your Privacy—The Reader Service is committed to protecting your privacy. Our Privacy Policy is available online at www.ReaderService.com or upon request from the Reader Service.

We make a portion of our mailing list available to reputable third parties that offer products we believe may interest you. If you prefer that we not exchange your name with third parties, or if you wish to clarify or modify your communication preferences, please visit us at www.ReaderService.com/consumerchoice or write to us at Reader Service Preference Service, P.O. Box 9062, Buffalo, NY 14269. Include your complete name and address.

HP11B

*Harlequin® Romance author **Barbara Wallace** brings you a romantic new tale of finding love unexpectedly in* MR. RIGHT, NEXT DOOR!

Enjoy this sneak-peek excerpt.

"IT'S TOO BEAUTIFUL A DAY to spend stuck inside. Come with me."

"I can't. I have to work."

"Yes, you can," Grant replied, closing the last couple of steps between them and tucking a finger underneath her chin. "You know you want to."

"So, you're a mind reader now?" The response might have worked better if her jaw weren't quivering from his touch.

"Not a mind reader," he replied. "Eye reader. And yours are saying an awful lot."

His touch was making her insides quiver. She wanted desperately to look away and refuse to make eye contact with him, but pride wouldn't let her. Instead, she forced herself to keep her features as bland as possible so he wouldn't see that a part of her—the very female part—did want to go with him. It also wanted to feel more of his touch, and the common sense part of her was having a hard time forming an opposing argument.

"If so, then no doubt you know they're saying 'remove your hand.'"

He chuckled. Soft and low. *A bedroom laugh.* "Did you know they flash when you're being stubborn?"

Rather than argue, Sophie swallowed her pride and looked to his feet.

"You so don't want me to move my hand, either."

"You're incorrigible. You know that, right?"

"Thank you."

"I still want you to move your hand."

"If you insist...." Suddenly his hands were cupping her cheeks, drawing her parted lips under his. Sophie's gasp was lost in her throat. As she expected, he tasted of peppermint and coffee and...and....

And, oh wow, could he kiss!

It ended and her eyelids fluttered open. Grant's face hovered a breath from hers. Gently, he traced the slope of her nose and smiled.

"Your eyes told me you wanted that, too."

If she had an ounce of working brain matter, Sophie would have turned and stormed out of his apartment then and there. Problem was one, she was trembling and, two, the fact she kissed him back probably wiped out any outrage she'd be trying to convey.

So she did the next best thing. She folded her arms across her chest and presented him with a somewhat flushed but indignant expression. "Do not do that again."

Will Grant convince Sophie to let her guard down long enough to see if he's her MR. RIGHT, NEXT DOOR? Find out in September 2012, from Harlequin® Romance!

HREXP0912